LOVE LANE

By Jack Marriott

Acknowledgements

Jamie Coleman, Toby Eady and Rob Warr.

Emma Steele

Catherine Lee

Thanks are also due to Martin Avis, Gina Dalton, Nick French, Alan Furneaux, Hannah Gerrish, William Holborow, Karen, Katherine, Alex, Miles and Steven Kearley, Miles Keeping, Stephen Lee, Paul McNamara, Daniel Rapson, Professor David Roberts, Frances Shiers, Ian Smith, Professor Christoph Tang, Robert Winder and, for the quote and paraphrased lines from *Double Indemnity*; to Raymond Chandler and Billy Wilder's screenplay; September 1943.

The statistics on heart attacks are a dramatic device and should not be relied upon. Although we have tried our best to catch any errors or typos, we apologise for those which may have been missed.

Love Lane

To my Father -

who loved a good story

One Chance to be Happy

It wasn't all bad news.

Yes, he would be working for the company again and burdened with their seemingly endless rules, regulations, Due Diligence checklists, protocols and audit trails. But then there was the money; God knows he could do with it, and it would be good to be away from London for a while. It was a chance to get out on to the open road.

He would drive west through the Home Counties and the chalk downlands of Wiltshire, then cross the granite moors of Bodmin to the treeless landscapes of the Penwith peninsular and he would do this part of the job at least, his way. There were things he missed about being a Company Man – a fat salary and a comfortable office, a Personal Assistant to do his bidding…but the sleek, German, company car wasn't one of them. On this trip, he would drive his gunmetal-grey *Thetis* the three-hundred miles to Cornwall and that would have lost none of its benefits. The progeny of 1950s Italian and English designers, she was part racy coupe, part comfortable saloon and he loved everything about her. The smooth curves of her quirky, characterful bodywork, the three-spoke steering wheel in

black leather and bright steel and her oh-so responsive
Alford and Alder steering. He had restored the car himself;
had nursed her back to health and knew all her secrets. Now
she was his forever.

But they would not be alone, the *Thetis* and him - sitting next
to him on the wide, tanned-leather passenger seat would be
Amelie Jayne Saunds. She was twenty-five years old, long-
legged and clever. And he would take her with him on this
case because he had been told to. On this case, he was
working for the company again.

It had all started the day before with a phone call from his
old boss, John Enson at *Hendersons,* after he had spent most
of that drowsy, late-summer afternoon drifting in and out of
sleep, trying hard not to think about what was wrong with
his life. It was just before five o'clock when he had looked
across at the woman lying next to him as she lay naked and
motionless under the white sheets and wondered what she
could possibly see in him. She had everything - he had
nothing. Although they had never talked about it, he had
always assumed that if she was here with him, she must be
very unhappy at home.

But he could be wrong. Perhaps he was simply an
entertainment for her – a must-have accessory for today's
wealthy woman about town? He fitted the bill perfectly; he
made no demands on her and had no commitments. He had
no money either and that too was good as he was never
likely to turn up and embarrass her at an expensive
restaurant or at a party somewhere. She came round once or
twice a week, they drank wine and made love then said
goodbye. It suited them both.

Lately though, things had begun to change. She had seemed
to want more from him even if it was only a sign that he
wanted more from her. She wasn't going to get it. He had

nothing left of himself to give her or anyone else and he realised that sometime soon, there would be a reckoning and he would have to tell her.

He stared up at the ceiling, lulled by the soft sound of her breathing and the murmur of the early evening traffic on Richmond Road.
'What's the matter?' she'd said without opening her eyes, '...you're restless.'
'I'm sorry. I was in a half-state.'
'You're a disappointment to me Tom - *I'm* meant to be the only thing on your mind.'
'It was you I was thinking about,' he'd said quickly.
'Oh good answer, *Dr* Rohm. Now tell me the truth – what's the matter?'
'I'm not sure we've got time *Mrs* Soames. When do you have to leave?'
'Not for an hour. You've got time.'

He'd got out of bed, rubbed his perennially aching lower back then put on his gown. He poured himself some more wine and looked out through the cracked window pane at the slow-moving Thames, noticing once again the flaking deck paint on his ageing, leaking houseboat. He told himself that he better do something about it soon or there wouldn't be a solid piece of timber left in the whole rotting hulk.
'If you want to know, I was thinking that I'm a disappointment to me too,' he'd said as he stared down into his half-empty glass. He looked up at her and saw how she had raised her eyebrows as if surprised by his sudden openness.
'Do you think we only get one chance to be happy?' he'd said, 'and if we don't take it, the green light changes back to red again. Is that how it goes?'

'I hope not,' she'd said. 'Some of us need all the chances we can get.'

She sat forward and reached out her hand but he'd offered only a thin smile in return.

'Come on - what's the problem? Tom 'Cool' having a bit of a crisis?'

'*Cool?*'

'You don't give much away you know. And by the way, you're still drinking too much.'

This was the moment when he finally decided she was getting too close; that she was beginning to acquire too many rights over him. At some point soon, this situation really would have to change.

'Let's forget it,' he'd said abruptly as he re-filled his glass. 'One more before you go? I've just remembered one of my clients might be calling round.'

'I don't want to forget it. Is this about us?' she'd said.

'No, it's about me. Me and my three friends – blame, guilt and fear.'

'You've been speaking to that wife of yours again haven't you?'

'*Ex*-wife. Ex-everything actually.'

'And you're still thinking it was your fault?'

'I've told you before, it was a cocktail of bad luck and bad judgment,' he'd said as he took another drink.

'Did you talk to anyone about how you were feeling when things started to slide?'

'You don't *talk* about things like that – English men just shut up and get on with it.'

Thinking back, how could he have been so self-pityingly maudlin? He closed his eyes at the shame of it.

'But now you have me. At least some good has come out of it,' she'd said.

There was a silence as he struggled to find the right words to say but he had been saved the trouble by a knock on the front door.

He had walked through the sitting room, passed the half-read books and the empty wine bottles to see the thin face of Tristan Caro looking in through the window. The man owned a local business and had recently hired Tom to handle an awkward little insurance claim. It was small-time and tedious but it was paid work and he couldn't afford to be choosy.

'I was passing so I thought I'd drop this off,' Caro had said quickly as Tom opened the door. 'I've decided not to take it any further - it's getting too complicated. There's a cheque in there for three-hundred.'

Tom took the envelope and frowned.

'Three-hundred? It's cost me more than that to open a case file on it.'

'Sorry,' Caro had said. 'Look, if ever any of my friends need help, I'll recommend you.'

'Don't bother. If they're anything like you, I won't be able to afford it,' he'd said as he closed the door.

Louise had got up and was dressing when Tom walked back into the bedroom.

'Sorry about that... are you off?' he'd said.

'I've just remembered - I've got to pick up the children. The Nanny isn't there this afternoon.'

She'd taken his hand and was kissing him when there'd been another knock at the door. Same door - different sound.

Even so, Tom had been half expecting to see Caro standing there, having changed his mind and now ready to apologise, but instead he opened the door to two men, one of whom seemed unnervingly familiar - he was small and sharp-suited and looked very expensive. Behind him, a much bigger man stood impassively looking on. He too was well-groomed but the effect was altogether different. He was tall and heavy and his large head sat on a pair of wide, square shoulders. He just looked dangerous.

'Did I get you out of bed?' said the small man, looking down at Tom's dressing gown. 'I'm Charles Soames. I think you have something in there which belongs to me.'

Tom looked first at Soames and then at the big man. No one moved.

'I'd like to see my wife,' said Soames.

Tom raised an eyebrow and smiled as if challenging them to do their worst but Soames just leant forwards and lowered his voice to a conspiratorial whisper.

'I know who you are. And I know the FCA wouldn't be happy to hear that you going around fucking your clients' wives.'

Then he stood upright and looked Tom straight between the eyes.

'When you were at *Hendersons*, you did some work for my firm. That's how you first met her wasn't it – at one of those client hospitality days? Where was it…Ascot? Henley?...'

Tom just stared back at him.

'…it doesn't matter. It's against your Code of Conduct and it'll get you struck off. Now, please tell my wife I'd like to speak to her.'

But before Tom could answer, a fully dressed Louise appeared and walked past the three men and down the gangway of the houseboat.

'It's all right Tom, I'll go with him. I'm sorry,' she'd said, before walking away along the riverbank.

Charles Soames had looked triumphant. 'You see unlike you, she's still got too much to lose,' he'd said with a satisfied smile.

Tom leant back, ready to hit Soames when the big minder jumped forward, pinning him back against the frame of his own front door.

'Now don't go losing your temper along with everything else,' said Soames calmly.

Tom had tried to push the man away but it was futile. As he shrugged resignedly, the bodyguard released him and turned to follow his boss, job done. When Soames reached the end of the jetty, he had turned and looked back.

'And by the way, this isn't the end of it...,' he'd said, '... there'll be more to follow.'

Tom Rohm closed the door, walked back inside and slumped down at his desk.

'Perfect' he'd said as he leant forward and poured himself a strong one; preparing for a difficult evening. He wasn't surprised when it was.

He tried to speak to his children but they hadn't returned his calls. His friends were all out of town and the pub had been empty. He was back home by nine and he'd even sat down at his piano and tried to play but his hands had felt tired and heavy. Then, just as he was opening another bottle of *Jim Beam* Bourbon, his phone had rung.

'Hello?' he'd said, not really caring who it was.

'It's John...John Enson, from *Hendersons*. It's been a while I know but I might have a job for you. Interested?'

'I might be.'

'There'd be some *real* money in it for you and it could get you back at the Top Table. It's the Sir Anthony Maier case. Ring any bells?'

'Died about six weeks ago in Cornwall...found in the street...heart attack.'

'You still read the papers then. Good. Well now we've got a tricky Life Assurance claim to deal with. I'll explain it all when you come in. How about my office tomorrow morning - around ten? You *do* remember where it is?'

'How could I forget?'

'I'm sure you've tried. I've got your web address so I'll send you the case files now. See you tomorrow.'

As he put the phone down and took another mouthful of Bourbon, Tom had felt a knot of trepidation in his stomach. He'd never really trusted his instincts but he could have sworn that out there, downriver somewhere, the warning light on a marker buoy was flashing. Was it because this was his first 'big-money' case since he left the firm or was it just the thought of working for them again? He didn't know. He and Enson had never really got on. It had been an uneasy truce at best and now, after three years without a word from anyone at the firm and after a visit from a vengeful husband, they call him at ten-thirty at night.

'*Tricky*...,' he had muttered to himself as he'd walked into the kitchen to get some ice, '...I bet it bloody is.'

A minute later he returned with a full glass and a lit cigar, sat down at his desk and switched on the *Apple G5*. It was time to find out more about Sir Anthony Mallord Maier RA; painter, sculptor, philanthropist and National Treasure...lately deceased.

Chapter Two

Back in the Game

Thinking back to that first meeting with Enson, Tom remembered how the feeling of unease from the night before had stayed with him as he locked the houseboat door and walked the familiar mile to Richmond station. His suit seemed not to fit, his collar felt tight and he had started sweating.

Forty minutes later, he'd emerged from Moorgate Underground and stared up at the Portland Stone clad HQ of *Hendersons Assurance*. Had he really worked *there* for all those years? It looked like a prison to him now. He had taken a deep breath to steady himself but had instead started coughing on the traffic fumes. Trying not to read too much into this bad omen, he'd managed to cross the traffic-choked road unscathed and passed through the revolving glass doors into the triple-height, marble-floored foyer.

It had all changed. The last remnants of the 1960s timber panelled interior had been stripped away and replaced by grey painted walls and halogen-lit, chromium steel and black leather furniture. The people seemed different too. The suits were smarter and the faces shinier but they were taut with the kind of nervous urgency which comes from knowing that your job is on the line every hour of every day, until you're either fired or hospitalised.

At the Main Reception desk, they were expecting him. He was handed a numbered security pass and a badge with his name neatly printed on the front and told to go up to the twentieth floor.

'Take the Express Elevator by punching-in the numbers on the pass then check-in again with the staff there when you come out of the lift,' the young woman on the desk had said with a fixed smile, hardly bothering to look at him.

He went through into the lobby and was just about to get into the lift when Charles Soames walked past him, deep in conversation with an artistic looking man with long, sweptback hair, dressed in a loose-fitting suit. Without seeming to notice Rohm, the men carried on talking as they hurried through reception and out of the building.

'Now what were you doing here?' Tom had thought. Was Soames still one of *Hendersons'* clients? If not, had he been to see Enson about more personal matters? He'd find out soon enough.

The twentieth floor was at the very top of the building and it was here that John Enson and the other Main Board members had their offices. Its dizzy heights were not for mere mortals and visits by the foot soldiers on the staff were rare. Even after he had been made an Associate and hailed as a rising star, Tom had been invited up to the top floor only twice in six years.

Having been borne smoothly skywards in the one dedicated lift which served this upper sanctum, he stepped out into the hushed atmosphere of the Executive Reception Suite as if emerging from a well-appointed air lock.

A large white oak desk had been positioned opposite the lift doors and at it sat the clear-eyed Gerry Eames – an east-ender in his mid-thirties who, it was rumoured, had at one time been in the SAS. Looking again now at his broad-beamed build and determined jaw line, Tom could believe it was true. Behind Gerry, a seating area of dark leather sofas and lush-green plants had been set out in front of tall windows with wide views out across the City of London from the Barbican in the west, to Finsbury Circus and Liverpool Street in the east.

'Hello Dr Rohm,' said Gerry cheerily as Tom handed over his pass code. 'How does it feel to be back on Mount Olympus?'

'It's even more difficult to climb than it used to be,' said Tom, pointing at his security pass and the cameras above Gerry's desk. 'Things have changed.'

'It was Mr Enson's idea. He designed the security systems himself.'

'It looks more like institutionalised *in*security to me,' said Tom.

Gerry smiled. 'I wouldn't know about that sir. Have a good meeting,' he said as he tapped in another code and watched Tom walk through the set of rosewood-faced double doors and into the office beyond.

This was the domain of the Personal Assistants to the eight members of the Main Board. Each one sat dutifully in front of their boss's individual glass-fronted offices, ready as Rottweilers to deal with anyone who dared to approach their master without an appointment. At the far end of the office was an unmarked door which Rohm knew led into the Chief Executive's office – he had been interviewed for his

Associateship in that very room. It all seemed like a long time ago.

Marie Stokes was John Enson's PA. As soon as she saw Tom, she had stood up and greeted him with a warm hand shake. She had always had a soft spot for him in the way a proud mother might indulge a talented but wayward child.

'It's *so* nice to see you Tom. How have you been?' she had said with a look of mild concern.

Tom had shrugged and smiled back at her.

'Oh you know - struggling on manfully. *You* haven't changed at all.'

She acknowledged the compliment then glanced over her shoulder into Enson's office.

'He's just finishing a call but do go in. Fingers crossed.'

Wondering just what she was crossing her fingers about; Tom had hesitated on the threshold for a few seconds as he looked in to see his old boss leaning back in his large chair, speaking on the phone. As soon as he caught sight of Tom, he had beckoned him in, gesturing to close the door and sit down.

John Enson brought his phone conversation to a close; his use of English characteristically economical.

'Yes…no…we'll have to bloody deal with that later,' he said as he put down the phone without saying goodbye. His expression mellowed a little as he got up from his desk and shook Tom's hand.

'I'm *so* pleased you're going to help us out on this. Have a seat.'

'I haven't said 'yes' yet.'

'I think you will.'

'How are the family John?' asked Rohm.

'All grown up. The youngest, Jessica, is off to RADA next month so I suppose I'll end up supporting her for the next twenty years. Bloody actors. I thought about trying it myself when I was her age so I can't really blame her - you've only got one life after all.'

'Luckily for some of us,' said Tom.

John Enson frowned at Rohm's distinctly un-corporate cynicism then walked across the office and poured out two glasses of mineral water. 'You got the files I sent through?' he said as he dropped two cubes of ice into each glass.

'I got it all.'

'So what do you think?' said Enson as he walked back across the room and sat down behind his desk.

'As well as acting for the family, your Fund Managers advise the Maier Foundation so I'd say you had some worrying conflicts of interest in paying out the Life Assurance claim.' Tom paused and took a sip of water. He could see he had Enson's attention but he thought he saw something else too. He had seen that look many times before; the narrowing of the eyes, that faint smile. Sometimes it had been directed at him and sometimes at others. Was it the look of a man who was tired of having to watch more talented rivals show-off and if so, why had he never noticed it before? He decided he was probably imagining it.

'It's a headline grabbing case,' continued Tom, '…a famous man dies in the street and there's a big-money claim from the wife. What is it - three-million? four? You're compromised so you need an 'independent' to look at it. That would be me.'

'Very good - almost full marks,' said Enson. 'The claim is for five-million, but you're right - the Foundation asked us to look after their investment interests and we shouldn't have. We represent the family too but with my connection to Anton and Miriam it was hard to say 'no'.'

'You were friends?'

'We go back a long way.'

'I didn't know that…'

'The point is,' said Enson interrupting, 'we need someone from outside the company for the sake of propriety. I don't want a stranger nosing around in our affairs so you're the obvious choice. You're still part of the extended family Tom.'

'Funny how it's never felt like that.'

'Do you want the case or not?' said Enson abruptly.

Tom paused for a few seconds.

'It'll cost you ten-thousand and I'll only give you two weeks. If I can't sign it off in that time, then bad luck. I still get half the fee. Deal?'

Enson looked at Tom then leant back in his chair.

'You'll tell me what's happening at all times?'

'Naturally.'

'*Naturally?* You're bloody joking aren't you - you never told anyone anything until you were good and ready.'

'I've changed,' said Tom, not really expecting Enson to believe him.

'I hope so. And just so we're crystal clear, make your enquiries with Due Diligence but without causing any fuss - then sign it off. The police are happy and so are we. Just go through the usual routine then get back to London.'

'I'll try.'

'You'll do more than 'try' or you're not the man for this job,' said Enson, his tone suddenly becoming hard and uncompromising. But then he smiled, leant forward and clasped his hands together in front of him.

'Look, we want to keep this low-key, okay?'

'Message received and understood.'

'And just to make sure everything stays on course, you'll take one of our people along.'

'Now who's bloody joking?'

'Company rules I'm afraid. It'll be one of the interns – only to observe. Her name's Amelie Saunds and she's on our Actuary programme.'

'Oh for Christ's sake John…'

'Stop complaining. She's clever, tough and pretty - what more could you ask for?' said Enson as he passed Tom her dossier across the table.

Tom glanced at the front cover then flicked dismissively through the *résumé* with its glowing references and photographs of her charity runs and enthusiastic fund raising exploits for various good causes. She looked painfully serious and just a little bit frightening.

'And she's still young enough to be optimistic,' Enson went on. 'It might do you good to be around someone like that for a while.'

Tom still had a resentful, unconvinced look on his face when Enson changed tack.

'It was your own doing you know – going off the rails like that. Was it me getting the promotion when it could have been you?'

'You were senior to me. It was always going to be yours,' said Tom, 'and just for the record, the Reuters case wasn't my fault. Files got deleted, hard copy disappeared and so did that bastard Jackson. Then Paul put himself in harm's way…'

'He's still with us you know. We found him something to do in the post room.'

'I try not to think about it.'

Enson shrugged and sat back in his chair.

'I'll copy-in Amelie on our emails and let her know you'll be going down to Cornwall…when?'

'Tomorrow. When the morning rush hour is over. I'll be driving down.'

'Do you still have that Vintage car?'

'Not *Vintage* – more *Classic*. It's a *Thetis*. A 1958 Pemuda *Thetis*.'

Enson nodded then walked across the room to refill his glass.

'If you pull this off, you'll be turning away work for years to come,' he said without looking up.

'And if I mess it up, everyone in the business will be turning *me* away,' said Tom as he stood up to leave.

'They're doing that already so you've got nothing to lose.'

'People have been telling me that a lot lately.'

'Then it's probably true…,' said Enson with another faint smile as he turned to look at Tom and raised his glass,

'…good luck.'

Chapter Three

Out of the City

So that was how it had begun. With a phone call from an old boss and a journey back to a place which was full of memories – most of them bad.

That evening, Tom was still angry at the thought of having to take the girl with him but he'd had no choice. At least nothing had been said about Charles Soames. 'Let angry husbands lie,' he'd thought to himself as he went off to bed. He would be away from London for a while and out of harm's way. Taking this case wasn't *all* bad news...

It was just after nine o'clock the next morning when Rohm wiped the condensation from the tiny porthole window in his kitchen and looked out to see a young, dark-haired woman making her way along the river bank. She was checking each mooring number in turn as she got ever closer. He recognised her from her photograph - it was Amelie Saunds. She was dressed in a grey business suit with her hair brushed back into a tight, neat pony tail and she was carrying a couple of smart-looking black travel bags with a red trim.

'Damn it – she's early,' he said to himself before a glance at his watch told him she wasn't early, he was late. As he opened his front door to her, he was still trying to get dressed. The top two buttons of his shirt were undone and he was holding a face towel in one hand and a fizzing glass of Alka-Seltzer in the other.

'Come in,' he said, trying not to appear too flustered. 'I'm running a bit behind. Coffee?'

His welcoming smile was returned with an expression which was a combination of strained politeness and irritation.

'No thanks,' she said as she came into what passed for a sitting room in the small houseboat.

'Sorry,' he said as he turned and hurriedly went back into his bedroom, 'I've got a phone call to make - I'll only be a minute.'

He closed the door behind him leaving her looking around the cluttered room with its rampant house plants and empty bottles of booze. A small piano stood against one wall with an ashtray full of cigar butts at one end of the keyboard. On a desk next to it stood photographs of two teenage children and a super-large computer screen displaying a complex-looking data analysis programme. All around the room, knee-high uneven towers of books leaned precariously.

In the bedroom, Tom dialled his son's mobile phone and waited.

'Hello,' said the voice at the other end, already sounding bored by the prospect of speaking to his father.

'Adam?'

'You okay Dad?'

'Actually I've got a bit of a problem for Friday.'

'No - really?' said the boy in mock surprise.

'I can't make it - something's come up.'

'What is it this time?'

'I have to go down to Cornwall – it's an important case.'

'I'm sure it is. I'll let Evie know you won't be coming.'

Then the line went dead.

Tom Rohm stood silently for a few seconds mourning the lost relationship with his children but then, resigned to living with his grief, shrugged, picked up his bags and walked back into the sitting room.

'Right, I think I'm ready,' he said as he emerged carrying his jacket and a small suitcase. Amelie was still watching the computer screen as the programme busily crunched through the pages of data.

'So this is 'claims central' - the beating heart of the Empire of Rohm?' she said in a flat tone.

'No - this *is* the empire. This is all of it.'

'How long since you started up on your own?' she asked.

'Three years. It's difficult to make a business like this work - there's a lot of luck involved.'

'And you haven't had any?'

'Not much. But I'm still here - just.'

She pushed aside an empty bottle and sat down on the sofa.

'You disapprove?' he said, catching her sidelong glance at the *Jim Beam* label.

'My father was a drinker and so were most of the men I grew up with.'

'I'm sorry.'

'There's no need to be. I'm sorrier for you – it looks like you're still in it.'

'It doesn't affect my work.'

'Well that's something,' she said, sounding unconvinced.

Tom sat down at his desk and turned his chair around to face her.

'Did you read through the Maier case notes?' he asked.

'Of course,' she said sharply, as if the idea that she would have been anything less than assiduous was unthinkable.

'And what did you make of it?'

'Straightforward.'

Tom nodded 'Yes – I agree. Pretty much an open-and-shut case.'

'*Pretty much?*' she said, 'A sixty-something man with a heart condition drops dead in the street. Death by natural causes - the coroner said so. It happens all the time.'

'All the time,' said Tom as he looked at her young face, so full of self-confidence. He'd forgotten what that felt like.

'And did you look at the Actuarial stats on heart attacks?' he asked.

'Should I have done?' she answered defensively.

'It's alright – it wasn't your fault. I don't suppose anyone at *Hendersons* even thought of doing it - that would have required creative intelligence…' He paused to check himself, aware of the bitter edge which had crept unexpectedly into his own voice.

'…I did. I didn't have anything better to do.'

'And?'

'Here they are,' he said, gesturing for her to come closer to the computer screen. Amelie got up and stood behind him, looking over his shoulder to see the databases and spreadsheets which Tom had opened.

'Do you know how many people have a heart attack in Britain each year?' he asked. 'It's about 300,000 – and of those, 106,000 die as a result. Seventy-five per cent of these are in hospital but of the 31,000 who aren't, how many are men in Maier's age-range do you think?'

'About half?'

'It's just over twenty per-cent – so about six-and-a-half thousand,' he said, scrolling down through the tables on the screen. 'And how many of them were men like him, with a history of heart problems?'

Amelie shrugged awkwardly.

'We know he's managing it. He's on medication, has a careful diet and regular check-ups and he's in the top socio-economic group don't forget – he's *Sir* Anthony Maier RA, not some poor bloke on welfare. The coroner's report tells us he's got no alcohol in his bloodstream, he's not overweight and he doesn't smoke. He's just walking in town one night. Now, how many men like Maier died in similar circumstances last year?'

Tom scrolled down through the tables then clicked the mouse and brought up the final statistic.

'One-hundred and fifty-seven. In the whole country in an entire year. So not as common as you'd think. But I'm sure our man was one of them.'

He looked up at her and smiled but if she was impressed, she didn't show it.

'If there was anything suspicious about his death, the police and the coroner would have found it. This is meant to be a routine case to give me experience – Mr Enson told me it would only take a couple of days,' she said.

'I hope you're right because the sooner it's sorted out, the quicker I get paid. Shall we go?' he said as he switched off the computer, stood up and put on his jacket.

Tom locked-up the boat and they walked across the island together under the willow trees to the narrow footbridge which would take them over the river and on to the embankment. A half-mile along Richmond Road, they turned down a side street at the end of which they could see a line of Victorian railway arches above a row of scruffy lock-ups. Two minutes later, at the fourth garage along, Tom opened the doors to reveal the *Thetis*.

'Proud Owner Condition,' she said.

It was the first time she had seemed even mildly impressed by anything about him. And was that a trace of deftly-judged sarcasm in her voice? Perhaps she possessed a sense of humour after all. If so, then there was still hope that the next few days would be bearable and that she hadn't been sent by the malevolent gods of bad luck to add to his pain.

'Will you be okay riding in this old thing?' he said. 'It's good for her to do long trips from time-to-time. It won't be as comfortable as a modern car but it's more fun and a little bit, well…nostalgic.'

'And just what is it we're meant to feel nostalgic about?' she said, now looking sceptical.

'The 1950s…motor trips on quiet roads in a less mad world…'

'I'll just do some work if that's okay,' she said, looking disinterested.

'Don't make yourself sick. Reading in a moving car can confuse the senses.'

'I never get confused.'

'Lucky you,' he said, realising he had been wrong to hope for better. This was going to be hell.

Chapter Four

A Journey West

They drove out into the morning sunshine with the car windows open and the radio on, taking the route of the old Roman road out of London. Half-an-hour later and clear of the traffic, they were cruising west at a comfortable sixty-five.

'So why go into the insurance business?' he asked her.

'It's secure,' she said as she looked down at the report she'd got out of her briefcase, seemingly bored by the predictability of his question, '…we'll always be in demand.'

'You're not one to take risks then?'

'I can't afford to. I've got people depending on me.'

There was an awkward silence for a few seconds then she put her work down and let him have both barrels at close range from her sawn-off shotgun of plain speaking.

'Look, we may as well be clear from the start,' she said. 'I didn't want this – working with you I mean. The Actuary programme is a great opportunity for me and I don't want it messed up.'

'By a has-been with a drink problem you mean?'

'If you feel you're not up to this job or you start losing your grip, you tell me, okay?'

'This is important to me too you know,' he said.

'I can see you need the money.'

'Then we should both be fine shouldn't we? We'll check out the claim, sign it off then come home. I'll get paid and you'll get the credit for babysitting me.'

She turned away from him and stared out of the window, shaking her head in disbelief.

'I don't understand why the firm hired you - everyone knows your history.'

'They were in a fix and I was their least-worst option,' he said.

She shrugged, unconvinced.

'We have to get through this the best we can,' he said. 'I didn't want you either. I'm used to working by myself.'

'Ah yes, the 'lone wolf' - that was a big success wasn't it?'

'For a while...' he said, pausing just long enough to allow himself a few more self-indulgent moments of regret. 'By the way,' he went on, 'we're going to have to stop for lunch. I thought at my sister's, in Bristol? The car won't last without a break.'

'You're sure it's not *you* who needs the break?'

'We'll both do. It's an age thing; the engine overheats and my back seizes up. Shall I put a tape on?' he said, fast-forwarding through her reference to his drinking.

'Please yourself; I've got some work to get on with,' she said.

'If you start to feel sick, you will say won't you?'

'Don't worry; I won't throw-up in your precious car.'

'Thanks,' he said, forcing a smile.

'Just make sure *you* don't,' she said.

They arrived at his sister's house in Bristol after a near silent two hours' drive, but Amelie was pleasant enough as Tom introduced her to his sister Elsa and her two daughters who were home for the summer holidays. The house was large, rambling and full of the signs of a happy family life and Amelie had immediately been made to feel at ease.

She was helping Elsa clear-up after lunch when Tom was dragged off into the next room by his freckle-faced nieces. The sound of a Bach Prelude soon drifted through, cluttered with mistakes and laughter. Every so often though, a passage would be played perfectly beautifully.

'Is that Tom playing the piano?' Amelie asked.

'Yes - he likes to help them whenever he's here. Lizzie's doing her Grade Five in October.'

'He's very good,' said Amelie with a look which bordered on disbelief.

'I'm sorry to say my younger brother is good at everything,' said Elsa, smiling. 'He won a scholarship to the Royal College of Music when he was ten. He had to go up to South Kensington every Saturday morning right through school but loved every minute. We thought he might take it up professionally but our father thought it was too risky.'

'I'm still new in the business, but he's not your usual sort of Claims Man is he?'

'There's never been anything typical about him, including his path into the business. After Cambridge he did some consultancy for the big insurance firms; Actuarial stuff for the most part to start with. He went to *Hendersons* on a six-month contract, did some claims investigation work and they ended up offering him a permanent post. After a year, he was made an Associate and being talked about as a future partner. It seemed that he'd found his niche.'

'And then what happened?'

'You'd have to ask him. For a while, people thought he was the best in the business and then…well, it was all very difficult. I think he had some rotten luck and they treated him badly. I still worry about him.'

There was an awkward silence.

'Rohm's an unusual name,' said Amelie, changing the subject.

'Dad was born in Hamburg but mother's English. We went to boarding school here – you know, one of those places which produces insecure children for ambitious, absent parents to fret over and feel guilty about...' she said, suddenly stopping speaking, hearing the silence next door. 'It's probably best to talk about something else...' she continued on in a hushed voice, '...Tom hasn't spoken to them in a long time.'

She had just finished her sentence when Tom walked back into the room. He went over to the fridge, took out a bottle of white wine and poured himself a glass. The two women looked at each other but said nothing.

'Lizzie's coming along nicely. She could get a Distinction,' he said.

'You play very well,' said Amelie, looking at him as if they were only now meeting for the first time.

'I'm a bit rusty, just like my boat,' he said, downing the wine in one large gulp as he gestured to her that it was time to go.

The goodbyes were heartfelt and Amelie seemed more relaxed as they set off. Tom had braced himself for three more hours of stony silence but even before they were clear of the outskirts of the city, she had started to ask him questions as if she'd actually wanted to hear his answers.

'So how did you used to feel when you set out on one of these things?' she said.

'I felt good if I was well prepared and edgy if I wasn't.'

'And which is it today?'

'It's all been so rushed that I'm not really sure. But at least it's an 'open-and-shut' case, remember?'

'What if it turns out that it isn't?'

'Enson told me to sign it off and get back up to London and that's exactly what I'm going to do.'

She looked across at him with one of those expressions which says 'now tell me what you're really thinking.'

'What is it?' he said.

'You think there's something odd about this case don't you?'

'It's nothing.'

'I want you to tell me anyway. You'll get tired of this before I do...'

'I already am,' he said quickly.

She looked at him for a few seconds, taken aback by his sudden brusqueness then turned away before reaching into her bag to take out her work. The atmosphere in the car cooled once more. After a minute, he cracked.

'Oh God, no more sulking please. You're the sort who never gives up aren't you?' he said.

'It's called *persistence* and that one quality alone can get you a very long way.'

'I wish I had more of it,' he said ruefully.

'I can show you how to get some if you like but for now, just say what you think about the Maier case,' she said, staring back as if daring him not to tell her.

Tom paused for a few seconds, feeling like an actor taking one final deep breath before stepping out into the spotlight again after years spent disabled by stage fright.

He had been so determined to do what Enson and the firm had wanted without asking any questions - to take a quick look around, ask a few routine questions then just pick up his money and walk away. Now, if he told her what he really thought and sowed the seeds of doubt, the facts would be re-examined, the evidence re-evaluated and alternative explanations would be sought. The idea would grow that the police, the coroner and the firm, may all have been mistaken. Yes, the case might indeed be open-and-shut and his suspicions unfounded; it was possible that it was all just as straightforward as everyone thought. Only he knew that it wasn't.

'Don't say anything…just keep quiet and drive…you'll ruin everything,' he said to himself. But before this sensible self could fob her off and move quickly on, the impulsive, unruly fool in him had shouted out from the back row.
'It's *probably* nothing,' he said.
'Then it won't matter if you tell me. I'm not going to…'
'The level of the Life Assurance is about right; around ten per-cent of the value of the estate,' he said, finally giving in, 'but the super-rich don't usually bother with these policies because they don't need the money and the premiums are too high.' Part of him was still hoping that these seemingly random, insignificant details would appease her curiosity. They didn't.
'And what else?' she said insistently.
'Anthony Maier didn't live in Polporth anymore. He still has a house outside the town but spends most of his time in America. It looks like he was only back for a few days.'
'So?'
'So statistically, there's a much higher probability he'd die in the US – he's there ninety-eight per cent of the time.'
'Is that all?'
'No. Rich and famous people don't usually walk around places on their own – especially at night. It makes them and their entourage very nervous.'
'Some do, surely?'

'Not Maier. By all accounts, he was a very private man and hated being recognised. And what the hell was he doing on Love Lane at that time of night anyway? It's a backstreet to nowhere.'

'Walking back to his car after visiting friends?'

'It would have come out in the Coroner's court – no one came forward. As far as we know, he didn't see anyone in town that night. The last sighting of him was by his gardener at six o'clock in the evening. The wife, Miriam, was out of the country so he was home alone.'

'And you're putting all this together with the heart attack statistics?'

'They're all low-probability events coming together at the same time. That sort of thing used to make me think I was missing something.'

'But they're low-probability, not no-probability.'

Tom paused for second then leant forward and switched on the radio. The cricket was on.

'You're right of course,' he said. 'It's best to ignore me.'

'Is this the Rohm intuition at work?'

'There's no such thing. It's Rohm's First Law. What most people think of as 'intuition' is the product of *analysis* and *experience*. The Second Law is that the best predictor of future behaviour is past behaviour and that's not the case here. Maier died because things which don't usually happen intersected with stuff he didn't normally do.'

As they drove down from the Mendip Hills and on to the Somerset Levels, Tom Rohm asked himself what had made him share his unsettling scepticism with a young girl on her first case. Perhaps it was the same reason science and mathematics had once fascinated him so - his unaccountable need to search out the truth and to look for patterns which would help him make sense of the world. But that had been

when he was a brave young man, full of hope; about a
hundred years ago.
He looked across at Amelie and smiled. Then, for the first
time, she smiled back at him.

Chapter Five

At The Schooner

They made good time after leaving Bristol and so it was just before five o'clock in the afternoon when the car rounded a high, tight bend in the road and Polporth came into view for the first time.

Looking down, he could see that the town owed its existence to the geography of the coastline. A narrow peninsular of land jutted out into the bay then curved gently back on itself like a maternal arm to create a natural haven from the storms of the Atlantic.

Stone cottages with yellow-green, lichen-covered roofs marched down sloping streets to huddle around a harbour full of lucent water and small sailing boats. High up on a green hill, between the harbour and the sea beyond, a stone chapel stood out alone against the sky. The church seemed to be watching over the old community; a beacon of faith down the centuries for the fishermen who ventured out on to the sea and a still sanctuary for those left behind to pray for their safe return or to mourn their loss.

As they drove down into the town, the gradient became steeper and so Tom took the *Thetis* smoothly and precisely down through the gears, slowing to a cautious ten miles-per-hour. Through the early evening shadows of the narrowing streets, he looked approvingly at the buildings around him. Most were made from the local grey stone with upper storeys of painted timber boarding or whitewashed rendering. There was little of the type of Victorian architecture he hated which, when overlaid with gaudy shop fronts, would put him in mind of an already unattractive woman who had then made matters worse by wearing too much make up.

Amelie adjusted her sunglasses, swept a few unruly strands of hair back from her face and took out the directions to the hotel.
'We seem to be going the right way,' she said with a look of surprise. 'Have you been here before?'
'No,' he replied, 'I memorised the map…' His words trailed off as he realised he sounded like a swotty schoolboy. He coughed and moved uncomfortably in his seat.

The buildings around the harbour were tightly packed together, most having been the cottages and sail lofts of the fishermen who, like the over-exploited shoals on which they had once depended, were destined for virtual extinction. The granite-paved streets and the courtyards where the catch had been salted and pressed now echoed the foot-fall of the holidaymaker and the second-home owner. But despite this, and because many of the lanes were impassable to cars, the harbour town looked the way it must have done a hundred years before.
As they drove along the quayside past the lifeboat station, surfers wandered back to their hotels and holiday-lets as

sailors tied up their boats after a day out on the flat sea. They motored-on past a pub with faded wooden tables outside before turning up a cobbled one-way street only just wide enough for a single car. After a hundred-and-fifty yards, they pulled off the road and stopped in front of The Schooner Inn, taking the last parking space in the small courtyard.

The Schooner was a three-storey building with white painted dormer windows set in a roof of blue-black slate. Steps led up to the front door which had a stained glass triple-masted sailing boat in the fanlight above it. A painted sign hung between the door and a bay window announcing that the hotel had been awarded Two Stars and that all rooms had TV.

'I asked Enson's PA to book us into something simple and out-of-the-way. That's how I intend to be whilst I'm here,' he said. Amelie looked nervously at him as if she wasn't sure what he meant but knew she didn't like the sound of it. There was a job of work to be done here and, as ever, she was going to give it her best shot.

They got out of the car and went up the steps into the dark lobby of the small hotel. In a tiny office by the front door, Tom saw a mousy-haired woman in her forties sitting at a desk. She seemed to be confused by something on her computer screen and didn't notice the arrival of her guests until Tom tapped on the open door. Startled, the woman looked up.

'Can I help you?' she said, her blue eyes darting back-and-forth between Tom and her computer malfunction.

He looked directly at her, making sure he had her full attention before speaking. 'The name is Rohm and you should have two single rooms booked under my name.'

The woman tried to open her computer booking system, failed, then dragged a hotel register across the desk towards her. 'Ah yes, Mr Romm and Miss Sands. Two rooms for two nights isn't it?'

'It's Rohm and Saunds actually,' he said.

'So sorry. I'm Mrs Trevenna, the owner.' Everyone smiled at everyone else. Tom noticed the faintest flicker of inquisition in her eyes. He decided that she was looking for signs of a liaison between her guests; either current or planned - a natural enough curiosity for someone in the hotel business. Amelie too seemed to have detected the tacit inquiry concealed behind the friendly smile and she and Tom had both shuffled uncomfortably without looking at one another.

'Breakfast is in the dining room between seven-thirty and ten,' said Mrs Trevenna, pointing to a brown door on the other side of the hallway.

'Would either of you like a newspaper in the mornings?'

'Not for me, thank you,' Tom replied curtly as he signed them both in. He reminded himself that he intended to work fast and that there would be no time to read the news. It would be a simple matter of going through the company's checklists and ticking the right boxes. Then he would drive back to London, write-up the report and get his money. What could be easier? It looked as if his luck had finally changed for the better.

Fifteen minutes later, Amelie was standing in her bedroom brushing her hair when there was a knock on the door. 'Ready for a drink?' Tom said as she opened the door to him. 'I was going to do some work...' she said hesitantly '...but come in for a minute.'

He walked inside, closed the door then stood waiting as she took the last few things out of her suitcase and laid them on the bed.

'I've got another report to finish but we could meet for dinner later?' she said, turning to face the mirror to tie her hair back into its customary pony tail.

'I thought we'd stroll round to have a look at Love Lane then go for a glass of wine. It's been a long day hasn't it?' he said, looking a little incredulous at the thought of anyone wanting to work when it was boozing time on a summer's evening.

'Alright then. 'Yes' to the first part of that offer but 'no' to the second.'

Tom shrugged then turned and opened the bedroom door.

'She misspelled both our names,' said Amelie as they went out into the narrow corridor. 'We've finally got something in common.'

As they went downstairs, he sensed a subtle change between them. It had been brought about by the intimacy of the situation – a hotel room, a man waiting for a woman to get ready; there were all sorts of associations.

He held the front door open for her as they went outside then stood on the top step for a few moments, breathing in the warm evening air.

'It's the quality of the light that brings them here you know', he said, looking up at the blue, cloudless sky above the whitewashed cottages set around the courtyard. Because the town had the sea on three sides, the intensity of the reflected light seemed to make the visible colour spectrum wider, revealing new hues in everything it touched.

'Brings who?' she said.

'The artists who live here – they've been coming to Polporth since the 1800s. Artists like to form colonies; Picasso in Paris, Monet in Giverny, Warhol in New York…I suppose they get to share ideas and of course, each other's partners.'
'Were the Polporth lot very bohemian?'
'Most, but not Anthony Maier. It seems he was the steady sort – wife, kids, sober and hard working. The other artists here were very unconventional - and deeply unhappy.'
'What makes you think that?'
'Apart from the in-fighting, the divorces and the suicides you mean?'
Amelie laughed for the first time since they'd met - a surprisingly girlish sound through a broad smile, as if something which had been locked away in her prison of dutiful, adult responsibility had momentarily broken free.

'For most of them, their personal lives were a disaster,' he continued. 'I suppose it's one of the occupational hazards of producing great art. Is it worth it do you think?'
She looked at him as if surprised that he could have such insights into the choices made by others when he seemed to have so little understanding of his own sorry state.
'I think too much time spent focusing inwards isn't good for anyone. And drinking makes it worse - people become morose,' she said. He had no doubt that this was another warning meant for him.

They set-off down a narrow cobbled street in the direction of the harbour, past neat cottages with white window boxes full of bright red geraniums. After fifty yards, the road rounded the supporting buttress of a high gable wall before continuing down the hill towards the quay. Off to their right, six steep, stone steps led up to what was no more than a path, just wide enough for two people to pass. Along this little lane, a short terrace of squat, two-storey cottages with pebble-dashed fronts looked out at a high, blank boundary wall. At the bottom of the steps, a street sign read *Love Lane*.

Tom walked forward and stopped at the foot of the steps.
'This is where they found him,' he said.
'The poor man.'
'He was poor that night,' said Tom. 'His fame and money couldn't help him; he was bruised, bleeding and dying. A man out walking his dog saw him lying here and called the ambulance but it was too late. They think he had his coronary at the top and then fell.'

Tom knelt down to look more closely at the steps, running his hand across the surface of the crystalline granite. 'This is unforgiving stuff,' he said, ruefully shaking his head. 'If wasn't dead before he fell, he would have been very soon afterwards.' He stood up and looked around. 'I suppose we better quickly check-out the rest of it – just so we can say we've been 'Duly Diligent',' he said, winking at her. She didn't smile back.

They climbed the steps and walked slowly along the lane. Tom looked carefully about him as if studying the detail of every house and shadowy corner. Old habits die hard he thought to himself.
In contrast to the promise of its name, the mean little street seemed like a cold, bereft place even on a summer's evening like this.
'I wonder why they called it Love Lane?' he said, speaking more to himself than to Amelie.
Each house had a set of steps leading up to a plain front door. There were no windows at ground level and only small, dark openings on the upper storeys, all of which were

shuttered closed. At night, the lane would have been lit by the single, ageing wrought iron street lamp which he could now see at the end of the terrace. Even if someone had looked out of one of the first-floor windows, they wouldn't have been able to see much.

At the far end of the row, they went down another set of steps and along a dark alleyway between tall houses before emerging out on to a sunlit cobbled street, busy with people. They turned left down the hill towards the harbour and walked along in the evening light, looking into the windows of the colourful craft shops and small galleries. Then, when they reached a fork in the road, Amelie stopped.

'I'm going back to the hotel,' she said. 'I really have to get on. There's a report to finish and revision to do for my exam in September.'
'Yes – I suppose so,' said Tom, disappointed but not really surprised at her continued lack of interest in early evening drinking. 'See you in the bar at eight? I'll find us a nice place to eat.'
'What did you think of the death scene?' she asked.
'I've done enough work for one day.'
'Come on – or I'll talk about it all the way through dinner.'
'You could try,' he said, but then noticed she had *that* look on her face. She'd had the same expression when she forced him to tell her what he really thought about the case and he knew she wasn't going to give up.

'Strange little houses and a sad place to die…' he said half-heartedly, '…and something has happened to the door of Number Four. Someone's locked themselves out or there's been a break-in. The door has been forced open and then repaired. It looked recent.'

'Why didn't you say something when we were there?'

'It's probably nothing.'

'You said that before. Would you have told me if I hadn't asked?'

'Possibly not. You can go back and look yourself if you want to,' he said, starting to walk off in the direction of the harbour.

'Wait a minute,' she said, running after him. 'Shouldn't we speak to the police about it? There might be a connection to Maier's death.'

'I shouldn't think so. Anyway, the police will have already checked that. We'll be seeing them tomorrow - it can wait until then.'

'But there's no mention of it in the Coroner's report…'

'I said it can wait…' he snapped. He stopped and faced her, his eyebrows furrowed into dark frown '…I'm off-duty now,' he said, looking at her as if daring her to challenge him again. Then he turned and walked away.

She stood there for few seconds, looking like a frustrated, humiliated child.

'Eight o'clock - downstairs in the bar. Don't forget,' she shouted after him, petulantly trying to regain control of the situation. But he just carried on walking, turned a corner and was gone.

Two hours later, Amelie was sitting in the bar of the Schooner Inn sipping her fruit juice as she glanced impatiently at her watch. It was eight-forty. She picked up her phone and dialled.

'Hello, faithful 'Watson', or are you my scheming 'Mata Hari?' answered a drunken Tom Rohm, audibly worse for wear.

'Where are you?'

'Why, what's the problem?'

'I think that should be 'Sorry, I'm late,'?' she said standing up and walking into the hallway, suddenly aware that her anger was obvious for all to hear.

'Oh Christ…' he said, looking at his watch, '…come down here then we'll go to get some food. I'm in The Lifeboat.'

'What lifeboat?'

'Not *a* lifeboat - *The* Lifeboat; it's a pub. Go down to the harbour, turn right and walk along the quayside about two-hundred yards…'

'Let's just forget it - I'll eat here,' she said, 'and in case you're interested, I confirmed the meeting with the police for tomorrow. We're due at the station at nine o'clock in the morning.'

'Okay, good…well done…we mustn't forget to take the case files…' he said, trying not to slur his words.

But before he could say any more, she had hung-up. She stormed upstairs, worked for two hours and then went to bed.

It was one o'clock in the morning when Tom Rohm found himself keyless and banging on the door of a locked Schooner Inn. An un-amused Mrs Trevenna answered in her dressing gown and as he carefully navigated his way past her into the hall, he was dimly aware of Amelie standing at the top of the stairs dressed in white pyjamas, looking down at him, stony-faced.

'We tell our guests to ask for the latch key if they're coming back after midnight Dr Rohm. It's all explained in the Hotel Guide in your bedroom,' said the hotelier as she turned and disappeared back along the hall.

'Yes of course it is. My mistake. Sorry we can't all be paragons,' he said belligerently as he looked up the stairs at Amelie.

He watched her as she turned away in silence and went back to her room. Then he heard the sound of a door close - not an angry slam but a detached, matter-of-fact closing of proceedings - the staccato click of resolute indifference. 'Bitch,' he said to himself as tried to walk upstairs, tripping over the first step. It was definitely time for bed.

Chapter Six

Meeting the Police

It was eight-thirty the next morning when Tom went down for breakfast, trying very hard to keep his balance as he attempted the difficult descent of the north face of the hotel staircase. He clumsily sat down opposite Amelie in what seemed to him like a particularly harshly lit and garishly decorated dining room and asked the waitress for water, strong tea and pain killers.

'Sorry about last night,' he said to his silent partner as she finished her breakfast without looking up at him. 'I'd been looking for a place for us to eat…'

'Don't…' she said, interrupting him. He stopped speaking and looked at her sheepishly. After a few seconds of strained silence, he opened his mouth to plead more mitigating circumstances, thinking she'd finished. She hadn't.

'…do that again,' she said. 'Do you know how pathetic you look in that state? You caused a lot of trouble in the hotel last night. The owner is still…'

'Alright,' he said, 'I've got it. I said I'm sorry.'

They sat in silence for another minute, not looking at each other, then Amelie finished her coffee and stood up.

'I'll meet you outside,' she said. Then she turned without waiting for a response and walked away.

The air was warm as they set off on the fifteen-minute walk across town to the police station and Polporth had already begun its daily routine. Shops were opening, awnings were being rolled down and pavements swept clean, ready for the day's business.

As he walked past the windows of the up-market High Street art galleries with their hand-made pottery and fine sculpture, Tom imagined Anthony Maier as a young man; walking with his artist friends along these same cobbled streets on summer mornings just like this. They would have been a striking-looking group; confident and self-assured, knowing that they were about to show the world a new way of seeing itself and change art forever. Then, still in his fragile, toxic state, he thought of the sad contrast between the legacy of those fearless pioneers and that of his own life. At times like this, after dark nights of soul-searching, he felt it was already too late - that he was holed irreparably beneath the water-line. But not content with that, he seemed to rejoice in waving away any helping hand as he slid under the dark waters. He stood still and closed his eyes.

'Are you alright?' said Amelie.

'Not really,' he said, opening his eyes as if awakening from a bad dream.

Their route took them through the old harbour town to the bottom of a steep hill which led up to the coast road. The buildings were more recent here and the streets wider and as they emerged from the deep shadows of the narrow lanes, the sun's glare was dazzling. A short way up the hill, they came to a small Art Deco cinema, its white stuccoed walls cracked and discoloured. Here, they turned off and walked down a side street which, after fifty yards, led them to a car park with three police cars lined-up neatly next to one another. They walked up to the front of the Edwardian police station, went through two sets of double-doors and into the front office. The decoration on the walls and ceilings was faded and the cheap chairs and blue *Formica* tables in the waiting area were chipped and scratched. Behind a long counter off to one side stood the Duty Officer. He was in his late-forties with greying hair and pasty white skin and he too looked tired and uncared-for.

'Good morning. We have an appointment with Detective Tallis – we're from *Hendersons*, the insurance company,' said Tom as he walked up to the chest-high desk.
The man looked across at his computer screen.
'Dr Room and Miss Sanz is it? You can wait over there,' he said, gesturing towards the shabby seats whilst at the same time reaching for the phone to call the detective. Tom looked at Amelie and shrugged. This morning, he couldn't be bothered to correct anyone on the mispronunciation of their names.

A couple of minutes later, a younger, more energetic man emerged. He was dressed in a dark suit and introduced himself with a firm handshake and steady eye-contact. This was Detective-Sergeant Rob Tallis. He'd headed-up the team which had investigated the death of Anthony Maier and Tom thought that he'd held on to Amelie's hand just a fraction too long before taking them up to the first floor and into a small office.

'I've put together the usual stuff for you – the coroner's report and our case files. You've probably seen most of it

48

already...' said Tallis as he passed a bundle of papers across the desk to Tom. 'So...what else can we do for you?'

'Not much – as Life Assurance claims go, this one is pretty routine. We'll only be here for a day or two and we'll try not to trouble you.'

'That would be good,' said Tallis with a humourless smile, leaving an awkward silence to hang in the air.

'There is one thing...,' said Tom. 'Miriam Maier - the wife - we've got an appointment to see her tomorrow. Is there anything we should know about her?'

'Yes - her husband died from a heart attack in July.'

Tom smiled uncomfortably.

'I have to ask the question. This is a substantial claim and we have to be sure there's nothing which has made you question her account of events. Some things can start off as unconnected dots but when you join them up, they can make a bigger picture.'

'I wouldn't know about that. We don't do much sleuthing around here, we just follow the evidence,' said the policeman.

'And what about the officers who went to Love Lane - did they notice anything unusual?'

'There was a body in the street,' said Tallis, looking across at Amelie with a grin. She could see he was starting to enjoy himself and she smiled back at him.

'Anything else?' continued Tom, undeterred.

'They were out on another call when they found him. A bloke walking his dog had called the ambulance but by the time it arrived, he was dead. I walked round there straight from home - I was on-call that night. I arrived four minutes after the station phoned me and no one had seen or heard anything suspicious. Mr Maier was in town one evening and he dropped dead. End of story.'

Tom paused for second and looked at Tallis. The detective was a handsome man but his face had become fixed like a mask, fired silicon-hard by years of exposure to the worst of the human condition. It had left him looking unchangeably cynical and perpetually mistrustful.

'Thanks. Sorry to trouble you,' said Tom gathering up the case files, 'we should go…'

'What other call?' said Amelie suddenly. 'Was it anything to do with the damaged front door we saw yesterday?'

The detective's expression changed as if he realised there might be more to this girl than he'd first thought.

'They'd gone to investigate a break-in at Love Lane,' he said, '– it's all in the files I've given you. Number Four has a silent alarm linked back to us here.'

'What was taken?' she asked.

'Nothing much; some cash, a couple of paintings, an old statue and a bit of jewellery. The whole lot wasn't worth more than a few hundred pounds.' Amelie looked across at Tom and was about to speak when Tallis cut back in.

'And before you ask, there's no reason to think there's a connection between Mr Maier's death and the burglary. We looked into it. It was probably just some kids on-the-rob – the owner was away. It happens a lot in the summer. He died of a heart attack with no sign that he'd been in a struggle.'

'He might have chased them,' said Amelie.

'He might…' said Tallis, smiling, as if she really was starting to impress him. '…but then we'd have to prove involuntary manslaughter without any witnesses. We're happy to leave things as they are to be honest. We don't have the resources to do any more.'

'But if new evidence was found?' she said.

'Then we'd look at it of course,' said Tallis with a slight frown.

'It's alright Detective,' said Tom, 'we won't be asking you to do any more work on this.'

'I hope not – it's crazy here at this time of year. The town's full of visitors and some of them cause us a lot of trouble.'

'We'll do our best not to become two more of them.'

'I'd appreciate that,' said the policeman as he stood up, indicating that the meeting was over.

'You're a doctor of what exactly?' said Tallis, looking down at the notes on his desk.

'Mathematics: *Probability Theory, Random Variables*…that sort of stuff.'

'That must come in handy when you're investigating a crime…from up there on the twentieth floor.'

'It has its uses. Some of it works quite well down at street level too,' said Tom, as they all walked out into the hall and went down the echoing staircase. 'Your accent - you're not local are you?'

'So you *are* a sleuth!' said Tallis mockingly. 'No. I'm from London originally. A long time ago.'

'How did you cope with the media after the death of a National Treasure right here on your doorstep?' asked Tom, ignoring the detective's sarcasm.

'It was difficult - particularly in the first week. But it's fine now. There's just the occasional pain-in-the-neck Claims Investigator to deal with,' he said, winking at Amelie.

'You're going out to see Miriam Maier you say? The Duty Officer here will give you the directions,' said Tallis as they arrived back by the front desk. They shook hands and said goodbye, then Tallis turned and went quickly back upstairs.

'So, what did you make of him?' Tom asked as they walked

across the police station car park and headed back to the hotel.

'A charming, clever, hardcase - your typical London lad.'

'He's certainly a hard case to read.'

'You'd expect that wouldn't you?' she said.

'Sure, he's a professional inquisitor so he doesn't trust anyone. It's just that, well, I usually get on with these people. We're meant to be on the same side.'

'He didn't think much of us did he?'

'He didn't think much of *me*,' said Tom, smiling at her.

'You weren't going to ask him about the door were you?' she said.

'I didn't need to because I knew it would all be in their case files and I thought things were going badly enough. Your pushiness annoyed him, in case you didn't notice.'

'I don't care. We're the ones responsible for the company's money; not him. And you know our Protocols – now you've got to speak to the owner of Number Four, Love Lane.'

'What the hell for?' said Tom, suddenly stopping and turning to look at her.

'In case the police missed anything,' she said.

'I wish I'd never made you think there might be something suspicious about Maier's death. Everything's there in the police file and if they're happy, so am I.'

'You'll get your money when we're *all* happy.'

'And when will that be?'

She leant forward and tidied-up the collar of his open-necked shirt. 'Look, the sooner you see the owner of Number Four, the quicker this will be over. Their phone number will be in the case files so you can call them and go round there this afternoon.'

'But I was going to go through the police statements,' said Tom, pointing at the files.

'I'll start on that – you go to Love Lane.'

'Thanks. What *would* I do without you,' he said.

Chapter Seven

Number Four, Love Lane

Tom Rohm walked up the steps of Number Four, Love Lane, sighed resignedly then banged on the front door with the curious s-shaped, wrought-iron mermaid knocker hinged on to the stripped pine. Its heavy thud echoed loudly off the stone wall opposite.

The door was opened by a woman in her early-thirties wearing a white cotton dress. She had arranged her hair so that the fair strands fell down over her shoulders, partly covering the silver chain around her neck and he found himself made momentarily speechless by her statuesque beauty. She didn't say anything but looked at him expectantly, waiting for him to speak.

'Miss Tessa Varle? I'm Tom Rohm – working for Hendersons. I phoned earlier,' he said, coughing a little as he handed her his business card. She glanced at it as she nervously touched the black stone pendant which hung from her necklace and then, without saying anything, opened the door to allow him to come in.

There was no front hall to the tiny cottage and so he walked straight into a fragrant sitting room with pale walls and rush matting on honey-hued, varnished floorboards. Two abstract oil paintings hung next to each other on one wall and a brightly coloured ceramic bowl had been placed on an oak coffee table in front of an oatmeal coloured sofa. On one side of the chimney breast stood a fluted Magistretti lamp and on the other, looking rather too small for the wooden shelf it was on, was a glass vase full of yellow Lilies. A roof-light was half-open allowing the warm afternoon air to drift into the room, infused with the scent of the flowers and Tessa Varle's delicate Sandalwood perfume.

They sat down opposite each other and exchanged awkward smiles. Tom opened his bag and pulled out the case file, putting it down on the table in front of him. He looked at her reassuringly but she avoided his gaze, instead staring down at the file.

'This won't take long,' he said, 'thanks for seeing me.'

'Is this about my claim?'

'No – sorry, I wasn't very clear on the phone. Your policy isn't with *Hendersons* – I checked. This is about the man who died at the bottom of the steps outside. He had a Life Assurance policy with us.'

'I wasn't here that night. I was away. I can't help you,' she said edgily.

'I know it must have been very upsetting. A robbery and a man dying outside your house on the same night.'

'Yes - it was a terrible thing to come back to.'

'The police have probably already asked you this but can you think of any possible connection between the two events.'

'No. And they didn't.'

'I'm sorry?'

'The police asked me what time I'd left the house on the Sunday before it happened but they would have known that already. I have to tell them when I go away because the alarm goes back to the station. Then I told them what had been taken. I don't remember them asking about anything else.'

Tom frowned.

'Did you know Anthony Maier?'

'I may have met him...he was still involved in the local art scene I think. Would you like some tea?' she said, standing up.

'Yes - thank you,' said Tom.

'He supported the arts here even after he started spending more time in America,' she said as she disappeared into the kitchen. 'I go to classes at the Art Centre every week so I could have met him...in the past perhaps.'

There was a long silence. Tom stood up and walked into the kitchen to see Tessa Varle standing quite still, leaning forward with her eyes closed, her hands resting on the table.

'I'm sorry,' she said, 'it was all so terrible. I don't like to think about it. I'm worried they might come back.'

'I'm sure the police are keeping an eye on the place,' said Tom.

'They promised they would but the alarm isn't working properly – I can't seem to set it.'

'I could take a look at it for you?'

'That's very kind,' she said. 'It's under the stairs...if you're sure you don't mind?'

'I like solving problems.'

'Then I'll make the tea.'

'It's a deal,' said Tom as he turned and walked back into the sitting room.

He opened the small stair cupboard to find not the simple home alarm he'd been expecting but the sort of top-of-the-range box of tricks he'd only seen used in expensive jewellery stores and museums. There were no visible sensors or audible alarms with this type of set-up; it worked using concealed movement detectors and tiny contact breakers on the doors and windows so only the most experienced thief would have known they were there. The system was designed so that an intruder would have no idea an alarm had gone-off back at the police station and so would take their time. There would be a better chance they'd be caught still on the premises rather than a ringing bell causing them to run off with the loot or being panicked into harming anyone.

'Who put this in for you?' Tom asked as he opened the cover of the unit.
'A friend arranged it all.'
'Well I hoped they paid for it.'
'I live here alone. They wanted me to be safe.'
'Well this would do the job. It's impossible to get past - when it's working properly that is,' he said as he began to run through the diagnostic sequence.
At first, the system behaved oddly as it went through a seemingly random sequence of file checks and deletions, before closing down altogether. Then, after thirty-seconds, it mysteriously re-booted itself and all seemed back to normal.

'Did the police touch this after the robbery?' said Tom, as Tessa Varle came back into the sitting room and put the tea cups down on the table.
'I don't think so.'
'And you haven't had the alarm people back?'

'No. I can't afford it.'

'Strange indeed. I'll just check the connections to the doors and windows. Is it okay if I wander around?'

'You're being very kind,' she said, seeming both reassured and a little surprised by the attention this man was giving her.

He walked through the kitchen and out into a small courtyard garden with white-washed walls and terracotta pots with blue and yellow trailing plants. In one corner stood a pewter-grey metal table with a single chair. It was a quiet, reflective space and the high walls and overhanging trees meant that the garden wasn't overlooked by any of the surrounding houses. Walking back inside, he carefully checked the contact breakers around the windows and door then went into the sitting room to find Tessa Varle reading and drinking her tea.

'You're sure you're not a robber too?' she said without looking up.

'With the premiums the insurance companies charge, some people think we are.'

'And what sort of insurance man are you, Tom Rohm?' she asked with a faintly teasing smile.

'When someone makes a big-money claim, I look into it.'

'So you're like a mistrustful policeman?'

'I'm a *Claims* Man – *Bayesian* statistician, psychoanalyst and tracker dog – all rolled into one.'

'And you investigate fraud?'

'We investigate people – "their twisted hopes and crooked dreams."'

'That's very poetic.'

'It's not original I'm afraid. It's from a story about a man who loses his way. He kills someone for the money and for a woman but he doesn't get either. He just gets caught.'

'*Chercher la femme*, Dr Rohm.'

'Thanks for the advice but for now, I'll just look for what's wrong with your alarm,' he said as he smiled at her and walked up the short flight to the first floor of the little house.

At the top of the stairs, there was a small hallway, just the one bedroom and a bathroom. All the rooms were painted in plain pastel colours and nothing hung on the walls. He checked the tiny sash windows; all of them opening easily enough to allow him to see that the contacts and locks were in good order. There were no obvious ways up from below and the courtyard garden would have been too difficult to get into. He agreed with the thieves - the front door had been the best way in.

Before he went back downstairs, he returned to Tessa Varle's bedroom to spend a few more prying, guilty moments in her private world. Her bed had been made-up with lace-edged, cream-coloured pillows and an embroidered white cotton bedspread. There were dried flowers in a vase on a wooden corner table but no ornaments of any kind; no photographs, bric-a-brac or keep-sakes. It was as if she had only ever had a life within these walls and he wondered who this 'friend' was; the one who had paid so much for the alarm to be fitted.

He walked back downstairs, opened the front door and carefully examined the damaged, dark wood of the frame. The repair had been done decently enough but the original break-in point was still clear to see. The thieves' technique had been basic but practised and they had known exactly where best to apply pressure to the door. It had only taken a single attempt. This wasn't the work of amateurish opportunists he thought and it would have been quiet and quick.

Finally, he traced the wiring back to the control unit in the cupboard under the stairs. There had been no attempt to tamper with any of the connections. Either they hadn't realised the place was alarmed or for some reason, they didn't care. He closed the front door and sat back down with Tessa Varle.

'Well that's as good as I can make it,' he said, finishing his tea. 'So where were you when all this happened?

'Dartington,' she said. 'I go there every year at that time.'

'In Devon?'

'For an art course. It lasts a week'

As she spoke, he found himself thinking once again how lovely she was - a woman who men would want to possess for themselves. So why was she unmarried and alone? How soft her pale skin looked. Would she be warm or cold to the touch he wondered?

'When you're here in Polporth, do you go out much? If the burglars had been watching this house before the break-in, what would they have seen?' he went on, hoping that his covetous thoughts about her weren't written across his face.

'I have a life drawing class once a week here in town,' she said, 'and I walk up to the chapel above the harbour most days and stay for an hour. Otherwise…I'm here.'

'Do you mind me asking what's so special about the chapel?'

'It's a place where I can look out across the sea.'

'And you go there a lot?'

'Every day if I can.'

Tom paused for few seconds then changed tack.

'Can you tell me about the things which were taken?'

'Two paintings and a small statue, three pieces of jewellery and twenty pounds in cash...there's nothing here of any value,' she said, looking down. The thought of it still seemed to upset her.

'I should go now,' said Tom as he stood up. 'If you think of anything which might link Anthony Maier with your robbery – just call. My mobile number is on the card. I'm just around the corner at the Schooner.'

'Thank you - I feel safer now,' she said as they went to the front door. Then she smiled, touched his hand and said goodbye.

As he left, he was surprised to find himself feeling just a little light-headed.

'Now that hasn't happened for a while...but don't get ahead of yourself,' he thought, dismissing the idea that he might fall for someone again.

Then, as he walked back along the lane, he passed a grey-haired woman who went up to the front door of Number Three. As he glanced back at her, she looked at him with what he could have sworn was a frown of disapproval.

Chapter Eight

On the Town

They sat in his room at the Schooner for the whole of the afternoon, dutifully going through the police files. It was the usual stuff and there wasn't much to be learnt from any of it. There were notes on Anthony Maier's movements in the days leading up to his death, the exact time the police had found the body, how the family had been informed, the post-mortem report…

It was around five when Tom finally closed the last page with a sigh of relief.

'Thank God that's finished,' he said. 'There's nothing in there. Happy now?'

Amelie looked up at him with the frown of a stern schoolteacher. There were papers all around her and she had been immersed in a book which Tom hadn't seen before.

'And you're sure Tessa Varle knew nothing about a connection between Maier's death and the break-in at Number Four?'

'The most interesting thing about the interview was getting to see her very expensive alarm system. I had to fix it.'

'You fixed her alarm?' said Amelie, raising an eyebrow.

'She's sad and alone there and the sort of woman who makes you feel, well…'

'Do I want to hear this?'

'I was going to say 'protective."

Amelie shook her head disapprovingly and returned to her reading. Tom got up, poured himself an early evening Bourbon, lit a cigar then sat down. He was restless.

'What have you got there?' he said to her.

'Press cuttings on the Polporth artists and a biography of Anthony Maier.'

'I think we did enough research on him before we left London don't you?'

'I got this lot from the local library whilst you were out 'protecting' Tessa. There might some things here which we haven't seen.'

'You're an industrious soul aren't you?' said Tom, ignoring the innuendo.

Amelie picked up the Maier biography, opened the front cover and read aloud:

"Neither genius nor education can take the place of persistence…and nothing is more common than unsuccessful men with talent."

'It says "after Calvin Coolidge". It was one of Maier's favourite quotes apparently,' she said. 'Who the hell was Calvin Coolidge?'

'He was an American President and a bit of a stiff by all accounts. When it was announced he was dead, someone asked 'how can they tell?'

'But he did manage to be President. Not bad for a 'stiff'. Just think what you could do with talent, education *and* persistence.'

Tom gave her a disinterested shrug then leant over, picked up the copies of the press cuttings and flicked quickly through them. As he dismissively dropped them back on to the table, a black-and-white photograph fell out of the bundle as if demanding to be looked at. He smiled at this apparent fateful intervention and duly picked it up.

The people in the photograph were posing like a family group. Anthony Maier was at the centre of the party – a dark-haired man then probably in his mid-forties with a confident smile. He was standing next to a woman who Tom took to be his wife, Miriam. In contrast to her husband, her face was sad; troubled even, and she was looking back resentfully at the camera as if it was a prying eye. Tom recognised three of the other people from his research as well-known Polporth artists - Edgar Rull, Julian Ashley and Vivienne Marchmain. Next to Miriam Maier was an older, Chinese-looking woman whilst on the extreme edge of the shot, a fair-haired, pale-skinned girl of no more than sixteen stood apart from the main group. Her face was slightly out of focus.

The text under the photograph read "Mr and Mrs Anthony Maier and friends at the opening of the Penrose Gallery, Barr Street, Polporth". The date on the clipping showed it was twenty years old.

Tom walked across to the window and looked closely at the image as if he was trying to get a clearer view of something. 'What is it?' said Amelie, looking up.

'It's hard to be sure but I think that young woman,' he said, turning the photograph round and pointing to the corner of the shot, 'is Tessa Varle.'

'So she did know him - she was lying then,' said Amelie.

'She did say she may have met him in the past.'

'You didn't tell me that.'

'I forgot. It's probably nothing - she could have just been there at the gallery opening - a coincidence.'

'You forgot? What did you say about low-probability events coming together at the same time?'

'I know what I said.'

'So what are you going to do about it?'

'Nothing. If there'd been more to it, she would have said or the police would have got on to it. Look, there's not much more to be done on this now. You only have to see Miriam Maier tomorrow and we're finished,' said Tom.

'I have to see her?'

'There's no point us both going up there and I've got to start on the report. It's alright for you; I've got to write this bloody lot up when we get back to London. No report – no money.'

Amelie stared at him in disbelief.

'You really are in a bad place you know. You're giving up.'

'You can't give up on something you never started - and I don't intend to start now because it's a waste of time. I was wrong to think there might be more to this case. My radar is a bit off these days. Sorry.'

Amelie turned away as if she couldn't bear to look at him. Tom walked over to the window, looked down into the street and sighed to himself.

'I know you're doing your best to help and I appreciate it,' he said, turning to her. 'We'll be going home tomorrow so how about a bite to eat in town later? It's our last night together.'

She gave him a half-hearted smile then gave a shrug of long-suffering acceptance.

Two hours later, they were chatting away happily enough over dinner as Tom resolutely steered her away from all talk of work whilst downing a succession of large Bourbons.

'Shall we go on somewhere for another drink? I fancy a change of scene,' he said as he paid the bill, making sure he got the receipt. This would all be on the company.

They left the restaurant and walked up the hill into the centre of town, past the busy hotels and packed pubs until they found themselves standing outside a scruffy, noisy bar.
'This looks pretty unsuitable but it'll have to do,' he said, looking up at the letters of the ice-blue neon sign above the door. They spotted a table in the corner so Amelie sat down whilst he got the drinks. At the bar he struggled to get served. 'It's not that busy', he thought to himself as his patience wore increasingly thin. Finally, he got the barman's attention.
'A glass of dry white wine – that Sauvignon on the shelf will be fine, a cold bottle of German lager – I don't mind which, and a glass of Bourbon please, with ice.' The beer and the spirit were both for him. The drinks were served with a slice of sullen indifference but at least he had them. As he picked up the glasses, a heavy arm pushed into his back and made him spill the beer. He turned round to see two young, drunk, twenty-something men, talking loudly to each other as they swayed closer to the bar, oblivious of the results of their clumsiness.
'I'm overwhelmed by the apology,' said Tom, pointing at his spilt drink.
'What's that mate?' replied the taller of the two, confused by Tom's language but able to translate his body language - they could see that he wasn't joking.
'You made me spill my drink. You don't have to buy me another but I think you should apologise,' said Tom, his eyes fixed on the tall man.
The two men looked at each other then back at Tom. Without warning, one of them swung a punch. Tom deflected the blow then grabbed the man's wrist with his left hand whilst at the same time, bringing his right forearm round hard, crunching into the man's jaw with his whole

body weight behind it. The lad fell backwards and didn't get up.

His friend jumped forward but his drunken lunge was stopped in its tracks as Tom thrust out a short-arm jab, fist clenched, into the lower part of the man's nose. He briefly staggered then collapsed back on to the floor and sat there spluttering, holding his bleeding nose.

Tom looked quickly around him, his eyes blazing. He saw only a stunned, silent bar full of people, too shocked to speak or move.

'I think you should call the police…and probably an ambulance,' he said, turning to the barman.

Then, as Tom turned to look over towards Amelie, a man in the crowd leapt at him from behind, pulling him down and smashing his head on the ground. As he slipped into unconsciousness, all he could see was a blurred rain of kicks and blows being landed on him from above. Then there was nothing.

When he woke up early the next morning, Thomas Newton Rohm was lying in a police cell; the smell of fresh bandages and antiseptic filling his swollen nose. He felt sick. Scenes from last night's horror show began to replay in his mind: regaining consciousness in that God-awful bar, being asked daft questions by stupid policemen then being taken to Accident and Emergency to get patched-up…

A quick self-examination revealed that he had a strapped wrist and he could feel cuts and bruises on his face and neck. His back pain had gone from chronic to acute and was hurting like hell. He was still trying to assess the extent of the damage when the cell door was opened by a very short policeman holding a very large cup of tea.

'Get this into you then we'll go upstairs. How are you feeling?'

'I've been better.'

'Your friend's here to take you back to your hotel. The tea's sugared but she's the one who'll need the sweetening. I wouldn't want to be you.'

Tom buried his head in his hands. He knew it was Amelie and what she would say. But he had it coming. He had it all coming.

Fifteen minutes later, he was taken up to a small, windowless interview room with a square grey table and three chairs. Opposite him, sitting impassively in judgement, Amelie and Tallis looked on unamused as Tom read through the statement in front of him. He frowned, shrugged and signed it.

It seemed harsh he thought; surely the lads in the bar had started it – he was just defending himself. But that wasn't how the witnesses or the police were seeing it. He was being charged with affray, assault and causing Actual Bodily Harm. The fact that he was drunk and the boys were in their early-twenties meant that things were looking bad for him.

'The barman said you can handle yourself,' said Tallis.

'I've picked up a few tricks along the way.'

'He was quite impressed. I'm not. To me you're just another dive bar brawler. I want you to take Dirty Harry here back to the hotel, finish your business and get out of my town,' said Tallis, turning to Amelie.

'I'm sure we're both very sorry for all this,' she said, now staring at Tom like an exasperated parent.

'Sorry won't do it I'm afraid. He'll have to come back here to go to court. They'll let you know when – it'll probably be in the autumn. Here's the bail form,' said Tallis, giving her the paperwork.

'It looks to me like he needs some professional help,' said Tallis impassively as he stood up and walked over to the door. As he opened it to leave, he turned round, looked at Tom and shook his head. 'You're a mess chum. You should see a *real* doctor.'

Tom stared at the floor. Tallis was right - he was a mess. His mind, his work, his family...everything. And he could find no excuses this time - there were no good reasons left to give himself another chance.

Once they got outside, Amelie walked quickly along as if she was trying to get away from him. She was frowning and tight-lipped as they came round on to the quayside but finally unable to contain herself, she turned on him.
'I don't believe it.'
'Would you mind not shouting please?' said Tom, putting his hand up to his still swollen ear. She didn't seem to hear his pathetic plea and continued angrily on.
'You were drunk, you started a fight and now they've charged you.'
'I didn't start it. And if I hadn't been pissed, they wouldn't have caught me from behind either. They really hurt my back you know...'
'You're an idiot! None of that matters - they've charged you!'
'I know they have. I was there, remember.'
'What's wrong with you?' she said, looking into his eyes.
'Come on - I want to know.'
Tom looked away.
'What started it – feelings of under-achievement? Passed over for promotion were we? Or was there trouble at home...?' she said.
Tom was about to speak but she ploughed on.

'Welcome to the club, poor little smart-arse Cambridge boy. Things always came so easily for you didn't they? Well now you know what it's like for the rest of us. We've all got crap to deal with but we don't hide from it inside a bottle.'

She took a step back from him, trying to regain her self-control.
'I hate your drinking almost as much as I hate your self-pity,' she said. 'You think there's something heroic about it all but it's just weakness. Underneath you're running away. I'm going back to London' she said, starting to walk away.
'You're right,' he said.
She stopped and turned to look at him. He had raised himself up and was looking straight at her.
'Right about what?' she said, as if daring him to say it out loud.
'About it all. I wasn't used to failing.'
'The real failure is giving up. Only losers do that.'
'I still don't know how it happened but I made a mistake on a case. Something got passed me and then someone got hurt. But they didn't fire me; that would have looked like an admission of corporate guilt. They just side-lined me then waited for me to self-destruct.'
'And you obliged them I suppose. What happened?'
'The usual stuff. Late nights drinking in town or at home downstairs alone. Then an affair, divorce, and then finally, I left the firm.'
'You jumped ship in the middle of a storm so you started drowning. You should have stayed and faced it down. Sometimes you have to be a tough guy.'
'So what do I do now?'
'You're still good at this business in case you hadn't noticed. Use it. Man-up and work your way out of this.'
'And you'll stay to help?'

'Why should I? You're a bad risk.'

'So demand a high premium.'

'You couldn't afford it.'

'Right now I'd be prepared to pay anything. Besides, you can't go back - the Maier case isn't signed-off yet and that won't look good on your record. If you go back to London now, you'll have failed.'

'No - *you* failed; I just gave up trying to work with you. The company will understand.'

'Will they? You were down here with me; we thought there was something 'iffy about the claim but when things got difficult, you gave up.'

'Don't try that…'

'The company only wants closers. They send their people out to bring back answers, not more questions.'

'I'm twenty-five years old and I'm only here to observe. I'm meant to be learning something from all this.'

'If you go back with the job unfinished, you'll be associated with a botched investigation. They won't care about your lack of experience - if you're good enough, you're old enough. If you stay, we can finish it. It's a chance to show them what you're capable of.'

Tom watched her brown eyes as she weighed up the options. The frustration and emotion of the minute before seemed to have been put aside as she coolly balanced what her head and her heart were telling her. It was a crossroads moment for both of them.

'You still think there's something odd going on here?' she said.

'There's more we need to find out before we can sign it off, yes.'

'Okay then. We'll carry on - but any more boozing and I'm on my way. That's the premium you'll have to pay if you want me to help you. No more drinking Tom, I mean it.'

'It's a deal,' he said. 'And what do we think of the probability of success?'

'No better than fifty-fifty.'

'That's about right. Not great but still better than it was ten minutes ago. Thank you,' he said.

They smiled at each other then turned to walk back to the hotel along the quayside in the morning sun. For the first time in a long time, he was sure about something.

High Cairn

Tom went up to his room for a couple of hours sleep to try
to shake-off the after effects of his night of shame.
He drew the thin curtains across the open sash window then
lay on his bed watching the cross-shaped shadow of the
frame as it moved slowly back-and-forth on the white
cotton. The still, warm air induced a half-state somewhere
between waking and dreaming and his mind slowly filled
with softly-focused pictures of cobbled streets and harbours
full of shimmering water. Then he imagined Tessa's face, her
lips slowly parting as she fell into his arms before her sweet
voice soothed him into a deep sleep.

It was almost noon when he suddenly awoke from a dream
he'd had many times before. He would fall from a high
building before hitting the ground with a jolt. Then, as he
stood up and walked away, he would turn to see that his
lifeless body still lay there. This time though, it was different.
The fall had been the same but instead of seeing himself
lying on the ground, there was only the faintest outline of

where a body had once been. This time he had lived and walked away.

He got up, shaved, showered, then went downstairs to find Amelie. This afternoon they would go out to *High Cairn* to see Miriam Maier and she would be expecting them. He would ask her routine questions about the Life Assurance claim and then ask some other questions which weren't so routine - about a Miss Tessa Varle of Love Lane. That, she would not be expecting.

Tom lowered the top of the *Thetis* so that they could feel the hot afternoon sun on their faces. After leaving the outskirts of Polporth behind them, they drove west along the coast road, bisecting a landscape of ancient field systems and wild heathland. To the north, a patchwork of olive-green fields separated by dry-stone walls swept down towards the sea and the white line of the coastal path. Southwards, the edge of the high Penwith moor with its granite crags and wild grasses rose up above them.

For the first four miles, the road ran parallel to the coast but then, in the distance, they could see that it turned sharply inland before disappearing behind a large white house which stood alone on a granite outcrop. The part of the house nearest the road was screened by trees but the rest of the building seemed to have been extended to the very edge of the promontory on which it had been built, looking out across the fields to the dark blue of ocean. This was *High Cairn*.

Tom started to prepare himself for what was about to happen; running through the questions he would ask and trying to anticipate every possible answer.

'Are you ready?' he said, looking across at Amelie.

'Of course not, I don't know what I'm doing,' she said nervously.

'You won't have to say anything, just look for changes in her behaviour. Help me to spot the lies.'

'But I'm not very good at that. Men lie to me all the time and I always fall for it.'

'That's because you *want* what they're telling you to be true. This is easier because there are no emotions involved. Watch her body language - it's all about non-verbal communication. Psychologists call it Neuro Linguistic Programming.'

Amelie looked back at him anxiously.

'Anyway, it's too late for all that now, we're here,' he said, slowing the car down to make the sharp right-hand turn off the road and into the driveway.

After thirty-yards, the way was barred by heavy wooden gates set in high stone walls which ran down both sides of the drive. Behind the walls, the Scots pine trees which had been planted along the whole length of the boundary towered over them.

Tom pulled up in front of the gates then reached out to the entry phone set into the wall and pressed the call button. After a few seconds, a woman answered and asked politely who he was. Her accent told him this wasn't Miriam Maier. He gave his name and although the woman didn't say anything, there was immediate buzz and a series of clicks as the gates unlocked and began to swing open. Tom accelerated gently forward over the crunching gravel towards the house they could now see fifty-yards in front of them. Its smooth, white-stuccoed elevations were only three-storeys high but the large chimney stacks and sweeping black slate roofs gave the building *Voyseyesque* grandeur. As they got closer to the house, a large, two-storey detached garage appeared off to the left, set back from the drive at the end of an asphalt track. Tom could see curtains at the open windows on the first floor and reasoned that this may have been a chauffeur's flat when the original house had been built back in the 1920s. He wondered who lived in it now.

They drove on, parked-up, and got out of the car. The pathway up to the front door was made of polished Blue Pearl granite flagstones, set in fine grey shale. All around, exotic-looking trees and large shrubs had been planted in naturalistic, free-flowing beds and borders.
Everything about the place was well-tended and well-heeled. The front door was made of White Ash and had a bright chromium steel handle at its centre. There were no windows at all on this front facade of the building – no way for the visitor to see inside. As they stood waiting for the door to open, light breezes circled around them carrying the scent of Mediterranean Fig and heady Jasmine, as if the house was already trying to cast a spell over them.

The front door was opened by a Chinese woman in her late-sixties who Tom immediately recognised from the photograph taken outside the Pendean Gallery twenty years before. She didn't say anything but smiled politely and made a welcoming gesture to usher them into the house.

The interior couldn't have been more different to the plain front of the building. Rich, deep-polished, dark oak floors and Berber rugs were the backdrop for the carefully lit Giacometti sculpture and the two large Rothko paintings which hung in the double-height entrance hall.
The housekeeper took them down a long, wide corridor with framed pencil drawings on the walls and into a huge room with floor-to-ceiling windows running along what must have

been the entire back of the house. The views out across the fields below to the sea in the far distance had been cleverly choreographed by the architect of the house; angling parts of the rear elevation so as to direct the eye towards selected features in the landscape - an ancient tree or a dramatic rock formation. The effect was mind-altering.

'Wait here please, Lady Maier will come soon,' said the housekeeper. Then she smiled, turned and left them alone.

Tom and Amelie stood close to each other as they looked out across a five-mile wide expanse of coast and watched the gulls and brown buzzards hover and wheel under the huge sky.

'So,' said Tom, 'do you think that living in a great house can help you to be a Great Man?'

But before Amelie could answer, a woman's voice made them turn around, startled, as if a spell had been broken.

'Dr Rohm and Miss Saunds - would you like some tea?'

It was Miriam Maier. She was a tanned, slim, sharp-eyed woman in her early-sixties, wearing a dark grey linen dress. With her large gold earrings and blonde highlights in her short cropped hair, she looked just as Tom would have expected the wife of a world famous artist to look – bohemian, stylish and very, very wealthy.

'No, thank you. This shouldn't take very long,' said Tom, extending a hand.

Miriam Maier smiled stiffly back at him. She offered her queenly hand first to Tom and then to Amelie before slowly gesturing to them to sit down around the small round table next to the windows.

'We're very sorry about your husband,' said Tom in an almost formal tone, 'he still had a very great deal to give to the world.' Miriam nodded in acknowledgment but said nothing.

'You have some wonderful art here. Those drawings in the hall…'

'They're by Moore and Sutherland,' she said, anticipating Tom's question.

'I've not seen them before.'

'I'd be surprised if you had. They've never been shown in public. There are many such works sitting in private collections and only the owners ever see them. Those were gifts. Graham and Henry gave them to Anton. So Dr Rohm; about our Life Assurance…?'

'Yes of course,' said Tom, getting the paper work from his briefcase. 'This is your husband's Policy. I have a few questions to ask you, most of which are simple confirmations. Sorry - company rules I'm afraid.'

'That's quite alright,' said Miriam as she leant forward to take a cigarette and a lighter from a silver box on the table. She crossed her legs and sat back, waiting for Tom to continue.

'There were no other medical conditions apart from those shown on your husband's last declaration; the Angina diagnosed ten years ago and the subsequent Coronary Stent procedure?' said Tom, starting to fill in the claim form as they went along.

'No,' said Miriam, lighting her cigarette.

'Had he been taking any new medication prior to his death or seen a doctor about any other problem?'

'Not as far as I know.'

'You took out the Policy three years ago. Can I ask why?'

'*Why*? I should have thought it was obvious. Most people have them.'

'With respect, when the Estate is very large, people often don't bother with them. It's rarely worth the high premium.'

'I thought we should.'

'*You* did?'

'Anton wasn't interested in such things.'

'And there were no intended changes to the principal beneficiaries of his Will?'

Miriam's expression changed as her body visibly stiffened. 'I'm not sure what you mean,' she said, seeming to bridle at the imagined impertinence of the question. 'The beneficiaries are myself and the Maier Foundation as they always have been.'

'Sorry, it's one of the standard questions.'

'There were no planned changes Dr Rohm.'

'Your husband wasn't planning to alter his Will in any other way?'

'Certainly not. Why should he? If you don't believe me, just ask his lawyer - he'd tell you if he'd received any instructions to change the Will.'

'You have different lawyers?' said Tom.

'Anton used another firm for his business interests so copies were held by both of them. What makes you think he wanted to change his Will?'

'I have to ask you - it's *pro forma.*'

But Miriam wasn't placated.

'Has someone said something to you? Did they suggest he might have wanted to change the Will? If they did, they're lying.'

'Nothing has been suggested by anybody,' said Tom calmly. Miriam was trying to rein in her anger but she was failing. It was as if some deeply buried emotion was on the point of surfacing but she was stopped from saying more by the sudden arrival of a dumpy little man who strode into the room as if he owned the place. Although he too was probably in his sixties, his unblemished, baby-smooth face and his black-dyed brilliantined hair made him look like a plump schoolboy stuffed into a businessman's chalk-stripe suit.

'I'm sorry to barge in Miriam, I didn't realise your visitors were here,' he said before turning to Tom and Amelie. 'You must be from the insurance company? I'm Patrick Devlin – Lady Maier's solicitor.'

They were still shaking hands when Devlin noticed the look on Miriam's face. 'What's wrong my dear?' he said, as he quickly walked over to her and put his arm protectively around her shoulders.

'We were just going through the Declaration form Mr Devlin,' said Tom. 'It won't take much longer and if Lady Maier has no objection, it might be a good idea if you stay whilst we finish off.'

'Yes - I think I probably should, now that you've upset her. In case you've forgotten, she's just lost her husband.'

'I'm sorry. I know it's a difficult time,' said Tom, 'but there are just a couple more questions to answer.'

Miriam nodded as she tried to regain her composure.

'You told the police that your husband didn't normally go into Polporth,' said Tom.

'He only went in occasionally; to see what the local artists were doing. We spend most of our time in America but when he was here, he liked to be near the sea. It was his inspiration.'

'But it wasn't unusual for him to be out so late?'

'He still had friends in town. I think he must have been to see one of them.'

'No one came forward at the inquest.'

'Then he was probably just looking at the work in the galleries. I was at our house in Greece and he'd just come back from New York. I hadn't seen him for two weeks so I really can't be sure why he was in town - I don't know why you think it matters. Look, I'm beginning to feel very tired. If there's much more of this, we'll have to meet again tomorrow,' she said, putting her hand up to her brow.

'No, I think we're probably done,' said Tom, completing the form and passing it across the table to Miriam. 'If you just sign at the bottom of the last page, we'll be on our way.'

As Miriam hesitated, Pat Devlin leant forward and picked up the form.

'You won't mind if I look at this before she signs?'

'That will be fine,' said Tom, 'but it's just the normal Declaration. I can pick it up before we go back to London.'

'Yes - from my office in town if you don't mind.'

'Of course,' said Tom, starting to collect his other papers together.

'There is just one thing more,' he said. 'Did your husband know a Miss Tessa Varle? She lives in Love Lane - where your husband was found.'

Miriam and Devlin both seemed to freeze for a second before Devlin answered, almost without thinking. 'No,' he said.

Tom raised his eyebrows and looked at Devlin as if to say, 'I wasn't asking you.'

'Lady Maier? Did you or husband know this woman?'

'No…I don't know. Perhaps. He knew people in town from the local art scene. I don't remember their names.'

'Just what are suggesting?' said Devlin.

'There was an incident at Miss Varle's property on the night Sir Anthony died. We need to be sure there's no connection between the two events…'

'This is ridiculous…' interrupted a now angry Devlin, '…you must have read the coroner's report. None of this was even mentioned. What are you trying to do here?'
'We're required to have all the facts.'
'If you're trying to delay or question the claim, you'll find yourself in hot water.'
'*Hendersons* aren't even thinking of challenging it at the present time. It's a simple question of whether this woman was known to either Sir Anthony or Lady Maier.'
'I don't know her and I really must ask you to leave now – I'm feeling unwell,' said Miriam. 'This has all been very upsetting'. She had closed her eyes and the blood had drained from her face. She wasn't faking, thought Tom - she really did look ill.
'Please go,' said Devlin.

Tom and Amelie left Miriam being comforted by a concerned looking Devlin and walked in silence back along the corridor to the front door. As they came into the hallway, the Chinese housekeeper emerged from a side room, smiled politely and showed them out.

'Well you certainly stirred things up in there,' said Amelie as they drove out through the gates and on to the coast road back to Polporth.
'It was more like beating the undergrowth to see if anything broke cover.'
'And something did. What's been going on to make them behave like that?'
'I don't know yet but it's a pretty big something – perhaps more than one *something*.'
'You softened her up with that stuff about the Will, then just when she thought you'd finished with her, you went in for the kill,' said Amelie.

'It's not that different a technique to a Lie Detector test. Plant the difficult questions in amongst the easy ones then look for the same signs the machine does – small but significant physical or psychological changes. I wanted to see how she would react to questions about touchy subjects.'

'And she reacted badly to the question about the Will and very badly to the questions about Tessa. They're both sensitive subjects then.'

'So it would seem. All we have to do now is find out why,' he said.

Tom drove along in silence for a few minutes as if weighing up all he had just learnt from his visit to *High Cairn*. He was smiling to himself, pleased with his afternoon's work.

'What did you think of friend Devlin?' he said finally.

'He's an inadequate. He's done well to end up as the solicitor of a rich woman,' said Amelie.

'Did you hear him arrive or see a car in the drive as we left?' said Tom. 'I didn't. I think he was in the next room all along and came in to stop Miriam saying something she might regret. We should check him out when we get back to the hotel.'

Amelie nodded in agreement then looked thoughtfully out of the car window.

'Hang on a minute, those questions about plans to change a Will aren't on any company forms I've ever seen,' she said frowning and turning to him.

'That's because I made them up. It did the trick though didn't it – she was completely thrown.'

'You can be a hard man, Dr Rohm.'

'Thank you. Now I remember why I used to like this job,' he said.

Amelie nodded then looked away; now it was her turn to smile. It seemed to be working. Thomas Newton Rohm was back in the game and playing well.

Chapter Ten

Some Background Reading

They had set up office in Tom's hotel room at the Schooner. Two chairs were pulled up to the small desk which stood against the wall, the Anthony Maier case files and the laptops were out and their mobile phones were at the ready.

Tom spoke to *Hendersons* back in London and asked Will Hough, head of the Search Team, to urgently see what he could find out about Patrick Devlin. An hour later, Tom called him again, set his phone on *speaker* then sat back. 'Okay Will, what have you got for us?' he said.
'He's a solicitor so that means there's plenty of good stuff in the public domain. He read Art History at Oxford before studying law at Bristol. After he qualified, he worked for five years for Kemps, the London lawyers. He didn't make it very far with them so left and moved to Cornwall to start up on his own. He wasn't doing very well at the beginning judging by the number of cases he's recorded as handling but he was also acting for Miriam Maier. Since then, the business has grown and now he has two partners and three junior solicitors working for him. They've moved office twice in the

last five years and he seems to get most of the criminal cases
around the town plus some bread-and-butter stuff – land
deals, commercial tenancies and a bit of family law. He's
unmarried, owns a fifty-foot yacht, the Kerkira, moored at
the Perkins Landing Hotel on the Karrack Islands and has
two homes in the Polporth area – a flat in town and a house
on Penwith Moor. I'll email all the details to you now. And
by the way, he was Best Man at Miriam and Anthony Maier's
wedding.'

'So what do we think about him now?' asked Amelie after
Tom had thanked Will and said goodbye.
Tom chewed his bottom lip pensively for a few seconds then
sat back in his chair.
'So after qualifying, he takes the usual young solicitor route -
he joins a big legal practice. The intention is to work his way
up but either he isn't good enough or he doesn't fit in. Then
he chooses this place to re-settle. Why? Because of his
connection to Miriam and through her, there's enough work
to get him established. He was best man at her wedding so
they're close. They go way-back and judging by today's
performance, he'll do anything for her.'
'And she's helped him be successful and own two houses
and a boat. Where are the Karrack Islands from here?'
Tom didn't answer. Instead, he frowned thoughtfully, picked
up the biography of Anthony Maier which Amelie had
brought back from the library the day before then went
across to the sofa and sat down.
'Sorry…the Karracks?' he said, already distracted by
thoughts of what the book in his hands might hold. 'They're
about thirty-miles south-west, out into the Atlantic. Why
don't you run some checks on Devlin's movements around
the time of Maier's death – just to see what he was up to?
You can use the firm's search engine; it can track credit card

use, travel, everything... The link is on my laptop – it's called *Loci*. Whilst you do that, I'm going to do some more reading about our dead genius,' he said, swinging his legs up on to the couch and stretching out.

Although only a short, two-hundred page biography, the recently published book had high production values and seemed both carefully researched and well written. It was candid, full of personal accounts and recollections and included many photographs of Maier's work and of the other Polporth artists and his close friends and family. It was the sort of stuff that he was now really interested in; Anthony and Miriam and their lives together - who this man really was. Perhaps if Tom knew more about how he had been in life, he might get a better understanding of why and how he died.

According to the book, Anthony and Miriam had first met in London at a Christmas party held at the Chelsea Arts Club. The event was being hosted by her father, Leo Heinemann, who owned a gallery in New Burlington Street in Mayfair. He was well connected, sat on various committees at the Tate and other London galleries and over the years, had become something of a rallying point for promising young artists trying to get established on the British art scene. Although Anthony Maier had already begun to make a name for himself through the work of the Polporth School in Cornwall, this was the first time he had been invited to Leo's at Christmas.

Maier had graduated from the Royal College three years earlier as the top student in his year and was already being spoken of as a rising star and the natural successor to Epstein, Nicholson and Hepworth.

According to the book, Miriam was, by contrast, feeling nervous about her future. She was in her final year at Oxford studying Art History and although her father's connections would guarantee a job in one of the big auction houses or get her on to a Masters course in New York or Boston, none of this had much appeal. She had grown up amongst it – the galleries and the exhibitions, her father's collector friends constantly coming to the house to talk about the buying and selling of art, which artists were up-and-coming and which had, sadly, already done their best work. She was bored by it all. She was particularly tired of the men who came to her father's parties – the artists and sculptors who often *looked* interesting but were invariably just posing. They were men who knew how to create the right effect with their art and in the way they dressed but scratch the surface and there was usually just a blank canvas.

Then, at her father's Christmas party that year, she met Anthony Maier. He looked interesting - and he was. She had seen him come into the room about an hour after most of the other guests had arrived. There had been light snow on that cold night and he had arrived, his face a little red, smiling broadly and still brushing snowflakes out of his hair. He seemed to be greeted by just about everyone in the room. At first, she had found the fact that he was so obviously the centre of attention both daunting and irritating and she had quickly given up being able to speak to him at all. Even if they were eventually introduced, she would be 'Leo's daughter and still a student'. He would be polite but quickly find an excuse to speak to someone more glamorous. In the event, he did neither.
Half-way through the evening, she found herself standing next to him and had surprised herself by taking the initiative to start a conversation. She had asked him what he thought

of the Hogarth print hanging on the wall just a couple of feet away. There had been nothing pretentious in his answer; just an assured, concise critique full of insight, humour and understanding of a fellow artist and he knew more about Hogarth's life than she did. She was hooked.

As the conversation went on, she realised she wasn't really listening to him at all, she was just watching him. He had a strong jaw line and high cheek bones and bright blue eyes with smile lines already forming at their corners. His face moved easily from the serious to the fun-filled and he was a man who took every opportunity to laugh.

As they stood talking, there were many chances for him to go off and speak to someone else but he stayed with her. Although only three-years older, he had none of the awkwardness of many of other young men she had met. This was a man who seemed to understand himself completely. He was someone who looked like he knew what he wanted and had the talent and ambition to go out and get it.

They started dating soon after that first meeting at the Arts Club. Over the next few weeks, they went to black-and-white, subtitled art-house films, watched the visiting American jazz musicians at the Scott club and of course, were seen in art galleries and at private viewings. He took her south across the river to his studio in Battersea, west for lunch on the Fulham Road and north for supper in Hampstead Village. They slept together for the first time at the flat he kept in Kensington on a wet afternoon at the end of January.

When they had been going out together for about a year, her father arranged Anton's first exhibition at the gallery in New Burlington Street. Although he was now becoming known on the London art scene, it was at that private viewing that Anthony Maier really arrived. His exhibition contained not only sculpture and paintings but also ceramics, textiles, theatre set designs and examples of his superb draughtsmanship in many charcoal and pencil sketches. But what really launched his career that night was not dazzling virtuosity, it was happenstance.

Leo Heinemann had dozens of contacts in the New York art world including a number of the curators of the city's major galleries. By coincidence, one of Leo's closest friends, George Brandt of the Museum of Modern Art in Manhattan, was in London to attend the opening of a Kandinsky retrospective which included works leant by his own gallery. Leo had invited Brandt along to see Anthony Maier's show before they all went out to dinner that evening. Accompanying Brandt was Robert Threlfall, the art critic and author, who was also in London to see the Kandinsky. As they walked around the exhibition, Brandt and then Threlfall, had stopped at one of the sculptures. It was a large abstract piece – almost four-feet across, superbly crafted in polished white bronze and cast in the form of a bird's wing. It was called simply, *Flight*.
On seeing it, they had both immediately thought of the work of the Romanian sculptor, Constantin Brancusi. Brandt's museum in New York had a piece by Brancusi and the two men agreed that the works could be displayed alongside one another – Anthony Maier's *Flight* paying homage to, and reinterpreting the work of, the early twentieth-century master. But they also both thought that Anton's work was a modern classic in its own right.
Brandt quickly turned to the exhibition catalogue to look for the price but a couple of other pieces had been added at short notice and so the catalogue had been hastily re-written. In the rush, the information on *Flight* had been entirely left out. It was a simple oversight but Brandt took this to mean

that Maier rated the work so highly that it wasn't for sale. This made him want it even more and so Leo was summoned to tell Maier of Brandt's interest and to talk about a price. Not imagining that New York's Museum of Modern Art would ever be interested in one of his works, Maier assumed that Leo was having a bit of fun with him and in response, jokingly said that he would let it go for fifteen-thousand pounds - the price of decent house in those days.

Before Anthony Maier realised the truth of it, Brandt had said 'yes'. There were some hasty phone calls to the trustees back in the States but the deal was done that evening. It was the highest price ever paid for a work by a new British artist and the next day the story was all over the papers - *"New York Museum Swoops to carry-off Sculpture by England's Young Genius"* and *"Flying High – Cornwall Artist Hailed as the Next Picasso"*.

As the plane carrying *'Flight'* back to New York took-off from Heathrow, so did Anthony Maier's career. Public and private commissions, international exhibitions and critical acclaim all followed. As well as charting his artistic success, the book made a point of highlighting Maier's talent as a businessman. He produced great work but expected to be well paid for it and some of his patrons were amongst the world's wealthiest institutions and individuals.

Anthony and Miriam were married six months after that first exhibition and the event was reported as one of the society weddings of the year. When they weren't in Cornwall, they lived happily in a large town house in Holland Park with Nina Choi, Anthony's housekeeper from his student days. Later, when the children came along, they based themselves full-time in Polporth where they bought and then dramatically extended *High Cairn*. Anthony still had a studio in Battersea and kept a flat in Notting Hill for his visits to London.

The rest of the book charted Anthony's Maier's rise to world-wide acclaim over the following thirty years and his role as a cultural ambassador for the arts in Britain.
Right at the end of the book, in what was really no more than a footnote on how the personal lives of the great-and-the-good had become increasingly fair game for the media in recent years, the biographer described an episode which made the hair on the back of Tom's neck stand up.
It recounted how Julian Ashley, an old Polporth-based friend of Anthony, had been prevented from publishing a book after a High Court Injunction had been served on him by the Maier family and Foundation. It was said that Ashley's planned book contained details of the private lives of the Polporth artists and that sections of it had originated from Anthony's letters. The Foundation argued that the letters to Ashley were intended to be private and were therefore not for publication. The court agreed.

Julian Ashley had been a member of the original Polporth artists group and Tom remembered that he was one of the men in photograph taken with Miriam and Tessa Varle. He also remembered that Ashley still lived here in town.

Tom finished reading and stared up at the ceiling for a full minute. 'Interesting,' he said to himself finally.
'No news of Devlin's whereabouts on the night Anthony Maier died I suppose?' he said, looking across at Amelie.
'You're going to love this,' she said, smiling. 'A Mr Patrick Devlin took the overnight ferry to the Karrack Islands from

the harbour at Fawler that very night; that's only a mile up the coast from here.'

'Even more interesting,' said Tom.

Chapter Eleven

At North Beach Studios

Although once famous, Julian Ashley was now forgotten by all but a handful of art historians and students of post-war British drawing. He was still regarded by some as an important figure in the development of the Polporth School but his small output of significant work had not been deemed worthy of even a modest retrospective by the major galleries. Nonetheless, Tom soon discovered that he was easy to find.

His website advertised the art courses he ran in Polporth and he seemed prepared to give lectures anywhere that someone would pay him to go. When Tom phoned to arrange a meeting to talk about Anthony Maier, Ashley said he would be working until late; 'just as I have done every day for the last forty years.'

Here was a man suffering for his art; a self-confessed martyr to his own cause, thought Tom. He disliked him already.

It was just before five o'clock in the afternoon when he left Amelie still reading through the police files to walk the short distance across town to North Beach Studios. The side streets were hot and empty and echoed only to the sounds of surf breaking on the nearby beaches and the cries of seabirds overhead.

Tom remembered from his research that the Beach Studios had a special place in the history of the Polporth School and that Edgar Rull, Vivienne Marchmain and Anthony Maier had all had spaces in the converted fishermen's net lofts which stood overlooking a sandy bay on the north shore of the town.

Studio 10 was hard to find but after searching the dead-end passages and damp, neglected yards, he finally found a pair of double-doors at the top of a timber staircase with a number ten painted on them. Underneath the number, a brass plaque read 'Julian Ashley RA, Emeritus Professor of Drawing at the Turner School, London'.

Tom knocked loudly then waited for what seemed like an age before the door was flung open by an intense looking man in his mid-sixties. Ashley seemed to have forgotten that his visitor was coming and hesitated before asking him in.

Once inside, Tom Rohm found himself in a cavernous, double-height studio space, lit by large, north-facing windows. The white painted stone walls were covered with rows of square-section, horizontal battens on which to hang paintings. There were half-a-dozen folding wooden chairs scattered around the room and a small sofa against one of the walls. In the middle of the paint-spotted floor, a large trestle table was strewn with bristle-headed brushes and artist's pallets covered in swirls of colour. Tom noticed that the colours being mixed on the largest palette corresponded to those being applied to what was one of the biggest painted canvases he'd ever seen. It occupied almost the whole length of a thirty-foot wall and must have been at least eight feet high.

Then suddenly, alarmingly, he realised that in one corner, sitting motionless in front of a deep-green backdrop was a very pale, thin, nude young woman. She glanced at him indifferently and then looked away.

'I'm sorry - I didn't see you there,' said Tom, embarrassed and unsure of what else to say. 'Is this okay – me being here I mean?' he said to her but the woman didn't reply.

'Of course it is - isn't it Gretchen?' said Ashley, moving quickly across to the trestle table and beginning to squeeze out a bright, Chrome Yellow ribbon of paint. 'She'll be quite comfortable I assure you. Do you mind if I carry on as we talk?' he said.

Ashley spoke hurriedly in a cultured, clipped manner at a pitch which was unusually high for an older man. He wore a cobalt blue polo shirt with the collar turned up in a self-consciously modern style, pale-grey trousers and white suede loafers. On the fourth finger of his left hand, a flamboyantly exquisite, silver and turquoise signet ring flashed like a Kingfisher as he twitchily mixed the paint on the palette.

Tom sat down at the table, frowning as he looked first at the painting and then across at the young model. For the life of him, he couldn't see how it was necessary to have a naked woman sitting there when the painting consisted entirely of abstract blocks of colour.

'She's the figurative grounding which I'm using to hold all these forms together,' said Ashley, noticing Tom's perplexed expression and guessing what he might be thinking. 'Do you see? The black line running down the centre of the painting is her profile. We've just started this morning,' he continued whilst introducing a little more white into the yellow block of paint.

'Do you have an interest in art Mr Rum or do you only like to talk about insurance?'

'It's *Rohm* actually – and yes, I do like art. Today though, I'm more interested in the artists themselves – dead ones in particular.'

Ashley stopped working for second and looked at Tom over the top of his glasses.

'Well then, we must get to point mustn't we...' he said.

'How can I help you?'

'I read about your court case - the one involving Anthony Maier's letters. I was hoping you could give me your version of the affair?'

'Of course,' said Ashley, now loading-up his brush and moving towards the canvas.

He began to apply the paint to a large yellow rectangle at the bottom of the picture near the base of Gretchen's supposed profile, continuing to speak as he worked the colour into the canvas with the stiff bristle.

'Anton had written many letters to me down the years and I was going to use extracts from them in a book about our little artists' colony here. I told him and Miriam I was planning to do it, just out of courtesy you understand, but she responded by setting her lawyers on me – first that idiot Devlin, then *Kemps*, the London solicitors. They were like a pack of Rottweilers and they tore my piss-poor provincial Counsel to pieces.'

Ashley walked back to the trestle table, put down his brush and sat down on one of the chairs. He leaned back, clasped his tanned hands behind his head and scrutinised Tom as if he was weighing up just how much of what he was about to say would be intelligible to a mere insurance man.

'Anton's letters were about being true to yourself and because he was, some people thought him self-centred and hurtful; callous even. But it was because he was a great artist you see - the usual rules don't apply. He had to follow his heart and desires. Such men can't compromise. As an artist, you're dead if you do that,' he said, eccentrically waving his arms about to emphasise his point.

'But that's not the way the world saw him is it?' said Tom, 'he seems to have been respected as a decent sort. Are you saying there was another side to him – that there were things he wouldn't have wanted people to know about?'

'They did a good job keeping it all out of the papers.'

'Who are *they* and what is *it*?' said Tom, intrigued.

'It doesn't take an art critic to detect cynicism in a work; a child of three can see it. Anton knew we artists have to be honest - always,' Ashley went on, ignoring Tom's question. 'He knew what the public liked so he didn't take risks, but he never compromised on the integrity of his work. He wrote about the creative process in his letters and they make fascinating reading.'

'But what else was in the letters? What were you going to say about Anthony Maier that people wouldn't have liked?'

Ashley eyed him suspiciously. 'I'm afraid I can't tell you that,' he said curtly.

'Personal things?'

'Some. I took them from the letters and my diaries. But after the court case, they can only be published when I'm dead,' he said bitterly.

'They didn't trust you to be discrete about private matters?'

'No they bloody didn't,' said Ashley, his face beginning to redden. 'They don't trust anyone and they don't like anything floating about out there which might damage their hero's reputation.'

'You keep talking about *they*?' said Tom.

'The Maier Foundation, his publishers, Miriam and Devlin…there's a lot of them on the payroll.'

'And not publishing those letters would have cost you a lot of money?'

'You're damn right it did. But I'm not finished – there are other countries where the lawyers are cheaper and the judges aren't so easily intimidated. There are plenty of jurisdictions where 'Saint Anthony of bloody Maier' isn't a National Treasure. I'm seeing if I can publish abroad.'

'That could be very lucrative; particularly now he's a *dead* hero.'

'And what's wrong with that? It's a fair reward for a lifetime's work.'

'So what sort of thing might devalue the Maier brand?' said Tom, beginning to see why Miriam might not have been so trusting of this old friend of her husband.

'I've already told you, I can't say.'

'Because of the gagging order or because it's a good story and it's worth a lot of money?'

Ashley smiled as if to say 'which do you think?'

Tom shrugged. 'I may as well go then,' he said, looking at his watch and standing up.

'I'm sorry, I can't tell you any more.'

'I understand,' said Tom, starting to walk towards the door. 'By the way, did Anthony Maier come here to see you on the night he died?' he said, turning to look at Ashley.

'No he didn't.'

'It's just that we're still trying to find out what he was doing in town that night.'

'Well he wasn't here. I hadn't seen him in two years.'

'And definitely not since you told him you were going to use his private letters to help you sell your book? He didn't come here to have it out with you - to demand his letters back and accuse you of betraying his trust?'

'I think this interview is over...' said Ashley, getting to his feet.

'Perhaps you met him in town and got into an argument in the street - in Love Lane even, then he had a heart attack and fell down the steps? Did the police interview you after his death?' Tom continued coolly, undistracted by Ashley's now obvious growing anger.

'You really are pushing your luck old man.'

'And you're refusing to provide information which may be linked to a man's death. We could have this conversation with the police present if you prefer. Now, I'll ask you again, what was in those letters and what were you going to say about Anthony Maier in your book?'

Ashley looked contemptuously at Tom then slowly sat down.

'Why don't you make some coffee Gretchen?' said Ashley, without looking at his model.

Tom glanced over at her as she got up, loosely threw-on a robe and walked out into a small kitchen at the back of the studio.

'You were about to say?' said Tom.

'That he was less than perfect.'

'Go on.'

'There were other women. Lots of them. Anton loved women and they loved him.'

'Who were they?'

'Take your pick, he fucked them all. Actresses, art students, models...in particular, one *very young* model. He was planning to walk out on his wife for one of them. National Treasures aren't meant to do that sort of thing.'

'How old was this model?'

'When it started – not old enough.'

'Who was she?'

'I don't know but she was special to him. He never told me her name - only that he'd fallen for her. '

'I'm not sure I believe you.'

'It's the truth.'

'Did Miriam know what was in her husband's letters before the court case?'

'She'd known about the affairs for years. As for him planning to leave her, I think she may have guessed.'

Ashley stood up and began to slowly mix more paint. 'Anton told me that staying with Miriam was killing him and that he had to go,' he went on. 'He said it was like the bloody *commedia dell'arte* in that house and that if he left, *Pulcinella* Devlin would look after her. The poor fool once even declared his undying love for her – with his predilections!'

'And who is *Isabella*? Who's the real love interest in this piece of theatre?' asked Tom.

'An educated insurance salesman; whatever next?' said Ashley, before turning and picking up his paint brushes. 'I've told you I don't know who she was. Now if there's nothing else, would you mind seeing yourself out?' he said as Gretchen re-appeared, took off her gown and sat down in front of the green screen.

'Thank you for being so helpful,' said Tom sarcastically, as he walked across the studio to the front door. Ashley ignored him and went back to work on his canvas.

As he walked back to the Schooner, Tom weighed-up the probability of Ashley still hiding something from him. The man was greedy and bitter and wanted to hit back at the Maier clan. He seemed to think they had it coming, but was that enough to have somehow got him involved in a man's death? But what about a jealous, heartbroken wife and her faithful servant – could they have been involved? Now that was something else again.

Chapter Twelve

On a Summer Night

'I think I'll go over to the Karrack Islands for a couple of days,' Tom said as he walked back into his hotel bedroom to find Amelie lying stretched out on the sofa. She looked exhausted. It had been a difficult few days and she hadn't really slept properly since Enson had first asked her to go to Cornwall.

'And I think I'll get an early night,' she said, yawning as she sat up. 'Why do you want to go there? The ferry will take hours.'

'You can fly there in thirty minutes from the airport at Larne; that's five miles from here. I need to find out more about friend Devlin. On the face of it, there's no link between him and Maier's death – that's the *null hypothesis* – but the more we find out about him, the closer he seems to get to it. He's at the centre of things we don't know about yet...' he said, sitting down, '...and its making my back hurt. I need to clear my head and get more facts.'

'What happened with Ashley?' said Amelie sleepily and with an apparent indifference to Rohm's plight.

'Anthony Maier wasn't quite the saint he seemed. It sounds like he left a trail of emotional collateral stretching cross five continents. He had a penchant for young ladies and at least one of them was a *very* young lady.'

'He was a dirty old man?'

'He liked them and they loved him. But one of them got under his skin – he was going to leave his wife for her.'

'Did Miriam know?'

'Yes she did. No wonder the Will was a sensitive subject – perhaps she didn't trust him not to alter it. So now we have a motive but we still don't know what for...sorry, I'm rambling,' he said, rubbing his tired eyes. 'That early night sounds like a good idea. I'll book my flight and the hotel, have some fish and chips then go to bed.'

It was just after midnight when Tom's phone rang and woke him from a deep sleep.

'Hello,' said a woman.

'Who is this?' he asked as he turned on the bedside light and sat up.

'It's Tessa. You told me to call if anything was wrong. I thought someone was trying to get into the house. I was frightened…'

His head felt heavy as he tried to make sense of what was happening. It was Tessa Varle - *the* Tessa; and she sounded upset.

'Where are you?' he asked.

'I'm outside.'

'You're here?' Now he really was worried - what the hell was going on? 'Wait, I'll come down,' he said.

He went quickly downstairs, brought her back up to his room then sat her down on the bed and poured her a drink. She was shaking and breathing fast. Rohm looked wistfully at the bottle of Bourbon and at the empty second glass then pushed them both away. 'A deal's a promise,' he said to himself.

'Are you okay?' he said, sitting down next to her.

'I heard a noise at the back of the house. I tried to tell myself it was nothing…but then I panicked and ran out…I thought they could get in,' she said, still hyperventilating as she tried to drink her Bourbon.

'But the alarm's working again Tessa – you're safe. The police would be there in a couple of minutes.'

'I wasn't sure what to do. I'm sorry. I should go shouldn't I? It was wrong to come here.'

'It's okay. Just sit and finish your drink then I'll take you home. We'll check the alarm and everything will be fine.'

'Thank you,' she said as she drank the last mouthful. 'Shall I have one more – just to help me sleep?'

'Of course,' said Tom, smiling as he stood up. He walked over to the bottle and brought it back over to the bed to re-fill her glass.

'You seem so calm; so sure about everything – I've never felt like that,' she said, sipping her drink.

'If only that were true,' he said, 'but you don't have to be sure of *everything* – just the most important things. I've only just learnt that.'

'What happened to you?'

He looked away for a moment and then, with a shrug of his shoulders, smiled back at her as if not knowing where to begin.

'Tell me,' she said.

'You'll be bored, I promise - there's nothing new about any of it. Something can hit you which you didn't see coming but then it's up to you to deal with it. I didn't.'

'I know how that feels Tom. I think that's always been my story and it's never going to change.'

'I think that we're all dealt our cards and there's not much any of us can do about that - but *how* we play them *is* up to us. That's about who you are and who you want to be. I found myself in choppy waters for a while — work stuff mainly, and it got to me. I lost my way. Steadiness is a much undervalued virtue. It's not fashionable to wear it on your sleeve but for a man, it's the secret of a happy life.'

'And is your life happy now?'

'Not yet but at least I've remembered what happiness looks like.'

'Can you help *me* to remember Tom,' she said, putting her hand on his arm. 'It's been so long...'

She touched his face then kissed him on the cheek and looked into his eyes. Then she kissed him again, this time softly on his mouth as she ran her fingers down across his chest before resting her hand just above his heart.

'Can I stay here with you tonight? Please Tom - I'm sure it's against all the rules but you don't always have to play their game.'

After they had undressed each other and lay on the bed, he ran his hands over her small breasts as he gently moved her on to her side. Then he kissed her neck and held her tightly as she drew him into her.

An hour later, as he lay awake among the shadows and the pale yellow light from the street lamps, he was sure of it – he was different now. He had sensed a change ever since Amelie had made him face the truth about himself and he'd seen his first believable chance of starting again. Whether this new journey would be with Tessa was a question he hardly dared ask himself but he would seek no guarantees nor make any demands. It was enough that she was with him tonight.

Just before dawn, she threw back the sheets and ran her tongue down across his body. When she was sure he was awake, she stretched up and kissed him on the lips as she lay on top of him. Sitting up, she gripped his sides with her knees and held him tightly in her soft, moist inside as he reached up to touch her breasts. Then, as her heart began to race, she fell forward to kiss him again before her passion gently subsided.

It was just after six a.m. when Tom woke to see her getting dressed.

'I should go,' she said.

'Yes - it's probably best. I have to go to the Karrack Islands today but when I get back…?'

'Call me. I want to see you again,' she said smiling as she walked over to the bed and kissed him.

'I'll take you home.'

'No – it's alright. I'll be fine now. But there is something else.'

'Just ask.'

'The little statue they took from my house – it meant a lot to me. Would you try to find it? Only if you get the chance I mean. It's a *maquette*; a miniature, of a girl - about twenty inches high. This is her…' she said, reaching down into her bag and taking out a small black and white photograph. It looked as if it had been taken in natural light, perhaps even by a professional photographer and it showed a white sculpture in sharp detail - a nude female figure in a kneeling position, her arms and hands raised a little as if reaching out in an embrace.

It captured such a tender intimacy that just for a second, the image took his breath away. The artist had caught the emotion of a moment immediately recognisable to anyone who had ever been in love.

'It's wonderful,' he said.

'She's made from Carrera marble but isn't worth much, except to me. Please try to find her.'

'I'll do what I can…she's very beautiful,' he said, still looking at the photograph.

Chapter Thirteen

Across the Sea

'I saw her leave Tom this morning,' said Amelie as they
finished having breakfast together, '…from my window. The
way you were after meeting her that first time, I can't say I'm
surprised. I hope you know what you're doing.'
'Probably not,' he said quietly. 'Let's not talk about it.'
'No one must ever know. It would finish you in the business
just when you're getting started again. I won't be telling
anyone but neither must you.'
He shrugged and said nothing.
'Come on,' she said, finishing her coffee and standing up.
'You'll miss your flight.'

By nine-thirty, they were driving in the direction of Lands'
End on the five-mile journey to the airport at Larne. Amelie
had looked pleased but surprised when he suggested that she
drive him there in the precious *Thetis* and then take the car
back alone to Polporth. He'd return on the afternoon flight
tomorrow and she would come to the airport again to meet
him.

Larne Airport was really no more than a landing strip in the middle of fields just inland from the coast. It consisted of two small hangers and a single-storey terminal; part of which was home to the local flying club.

As he boarded the plane and lowered himself slowly into his cramped seat, he had a contented smile on his face. Last night, he had made love with a beautiful woman and now he would fly to a place he had never been to before. He had always loved journeys, no matter how short. During this precious time, no one could get to him and, best of all, he didn't have to feel guilty about doing precisely *nothing*. For once, he had the time and the space to reflect and to ponder and it felt to him like freedom.

The thirty-seater aeroplane took off on time then banked around to the south-west to swing out over the flat sea. As they crossed the Cornish coastline, Tom looked down to see an open-air theatre, cut high into the grey cliffs. He remembered reading about its history and how it had been designed as a miniature Greek-style amphitheatre with the sea as the backdrop to the stage. It had been built by an English spinster and her handful of gardeners during the 1930s. Short of money and battling against the elements, they had moved all the necessary construction materials; the structural timbers, the beams, blocks, lintels, brick, cement and stone – by hand and wooden wheelbarrow, up and down the crude steps and pathways, year-after-year until it was done.

It was a beguiling story of the power of dreams, love and, as Amelie would have pointed out, *persistence*.

As the theatre disappeared from view, a slender, gently tapering lighthouse could be seen standing resolutely in the middle of the *Mer Diroise* – the 'Angry Sea'; the meeting point of the currents and deep swells of the Irish Sea, the

English Channel and the Atlantic Ocean. Built on a
protruding plug of volcanic lava, the hundred-foot high
tower had been finished in the 1860s and had needed four-
thousand tonnes of ingeniously rebated masonry to be
carried out across the sea for its making.

Tom thought of the courage of the men who had raised it
and of those who had then lived in its storm-battered
isolation in the long years before automation. How pitiful his
recent trials had been in comparison with theirs and how
ashamed he should feel of his meagre efforts in the face of
such trivial adversity.

Twenty minutes later, just as the plane began its final descent
to the islands, they flew over a dozen slate-black Basking
Sharks, each about thirty-feet long and all facing the same
direction, just beneath the surface. They didn't have to do
very much, he thought; just make sure that they were in the
right place then open the door and wait for the food to drift
in. But the real skill of it, the difficult thing which made it
look easy, was the *analysis*; of the water temperature, of its
constituents, and of the currents and the direction in which
they moved. Get all of that right and these gentle giants
could home-in across vast distances on the plankton blooms
on which they fed. But get the analysis wrong and you could
be waiting for your lunch indefinitely, forever in the wrong
place.

These were lessons of his mini-travelogue he thought.
'Analysis, courage, persistence…' he whispered, mantra-like,
to himself.

The Karracks were an archipelago of about forty granite
islands set around shallow lagoons of bright blue and
turquoise water. Although St Mawe, where the ferries from
the mainland docked, was a large, thriving town, many of the
outer isles were no more than bare black rock and home

only to nesting sea birds. As they drew closer and he looked down on the shores which faced the mainland, waves could be seen gently breaking onto sandy beaches but on the rocky coastlines which faced west, the full force of the Atlantic crashed in.

Before the great thaw at the end of the Ice Age, the water level of the Atlantic had been thirty-feet lower than it was now and today's Karracks were all that remained of a much larger area which had been covered with ancient field systems and settlements. At low tide, many of the islands were temporarily re-connected to each other and as the plane flew in to land, the forlorn remains of Neolithic standing stones and burial chambers could be seen dotted across the exposed sea bed and sandbars.

The aeroplane touched gently down on a landing strip between yellow fields, low hedgerows and narrow country roads. A small bus took them from the airport into the town and on to the harbour for those making connections by boat to the other islands. Within a few minutes of arriving on the dockside, Tom was walking down the slippery stone steps next to the harbour wall and on to the motor launch which was to take him to the outlying island of Tremorna.

The small boat chugged slowly across the shallow harbour, past the town beach and its Napoleonic fort and out into the swirling open water. For the next half-hour the skipper skilfully navigated between the rocks and sandbanks as he dropped-off his passengers at the landing stages on the different islands.

As they approached Tremorna, Tom could see two men waiting at the end of a long jetty which ran fifty-yards out into the sea over a shallow slope of white sand.

Once they were securely tied-up, Tom and five other passengers stepped out of the boat, helped by the two men, both of whom wore dark-blue sweatshirts which had small, yellow *PLH* logos. He realised they were from the hotel, sent to shepherd home the new arrivals.

They all trooped along the wooden slatted walkway as it weaved its way across the dunes and up to a dusty brown concrete road above the beach. There were no cars on the island and so transport was either by bicycle or, for guests of the hotel, by tractor-towed trailer which had seats for ten under a large green canvas canopy.

Standing in the strong sun as the luggage was stowed under the rows of leather upholstered benches, the skin on Tom's face and arms started to tighten. These exposed islands were after all, in the Atlantic Ocean and it was beginning to feel like he was actually out at sea and being weather beaten by hot, salt-laden air.

He clambered unsteadily up to take his seat before the tractor started off with a lurch then crawled noisily inland down narrow lanes.

There were no houses along the way, just fields, rolling hills and constant views of the sea. At one point, the road passed a cricket pitch with a small pavilion off to one side. He was thinking how out of place it seemed in this remote island landscape, when he turned to see a large helicopter coming into land on the outfield, bringing more guests to the hotel and the time-share homes on the island. There were no bed-and-breakfasts, campsites or caravans on Tremorna and few properties to rent. Rooms at both of the hotels were expensive and it was to the pricier of the two that he was going. It was here that Pat Devlin moored his boat.

A mile further on and the road ran down once more to the water's edge. After following the shore line for about a hundred yards, they passed through an open set of low gates and into the grounds of the hotel before coming to a standstill in front of the entrance.

The hotel's façade was of grey stone and shiplap wooden boarding punctuated with dramatic floor-to-ceiling windows. The timber of the surrounding decks and walkways had been allowed to bleach-out in the strong sun and so was coated in a silver-white patina. There was no signage at all on the front of the main building; no names or Star Ratings - just a small brass plate next to the entrance which read *Perkins Landing*. This was a hotel which didn't need to advertise itself.

Tom and the other guests were helped down from the trailer and shown into reception as their baggage was unloaded. The floor of the entrance lobby was of grey-green slate and the walls were hung with large paintings depicting the island's unspoilt white beaches. Off to one side of the front desk, glass cabinets displayed the local aquamarine and yellow pottery.

Tom was checked-in by a young woman in a dark-blue blouse before he was shown to his room by the hotel manager. The man chatted politely as he took Tom along the wide, quiet corridors with their storey-height windows and open views of the sea and, to the landward side, of the sub-tropical plants in the hotel gardens.

The manager unlocked the door to Room Twelve and they went through a small lobby area into a large suite, the upper part of which was almost entirely filled by a king-size bed. Beyond the sleeping area, three carpeted steps led down to a lower living space with a long sofa, wide armchairs and a huge wall-mounted Television. Fresh flowers and a half-bottle of *Moet*, chilling in a glass ice-bowl, sat on the coffee table in front of the sofa. The whole of the end wall of the room was glazed; sections of which could be opened to allow the guest out on to a private terrace which overlooked a sandy bay.

When the manager had gone, Tom unpacked and, armed with a guidebook he had picked up in Reception, went to have coffee out on one of the terraces. He sat at an empty table under a white canvas parasol and looked out across the sea towards the four other islands which could be seen running in a line southwards along the horizon. Their shorelines were over two miles away and indistinct in the heat haze of the morning, but beyond the faint yellow line of their beaches, green fields could be seen sweeping up to high, stony ridges of dark granite.

Off to the right of the terrace, the hotel gardens ended in a low, drystone wall. Beyond that and next to a concrete slipway which led down to the beach stood a single-storey wooden hut with a hand-painted hanging sign which read "Old Landing Sailing Club" written in white letters.
On the beach, the *Toppers, Mirrors* and *Lasers* used to teach beginners how to sail, lay tilted over on the sand, tethered to their exposed mooring ropes. Apart from a young couple with two small children who were lying quietly in the hot sun on blue-and-yellow beach towels, the bay was entirely empty of people. The bright sun, the deep turquoise of the sea and the crystalline, iridescent quality of the sand put him more in mind of the islands of the Indian Ocean than of the north Atlantic. This place was a well-kept secret, he thought.

About halfway along the beach, set back from the road, stood four large Victorian stone houses. According to his island guidebook, these were *timeshares* and to buy the right to spend a week every year in one of these houses could cost upwards of £200,000 for a twenty-year lease, depending on size and position. It was also possible to moor a boat here then use the facilities of the hotel and the bookings and payments for this service were organised through the sailing club. This, he knew, was the very arrangement which Pat Devlin had been using for the past five years.

The guidebook also said that the club, the hotels and the Freeholds of all of the houses belonged to a single family who, therefore, effectively owned the whole island. There were strict rules about how the place was to be kept looking this idyllic and how everyone should behave. Apparently, there were no Residents Associations, Boards or Committees and no compromises or appeals were possible or necessary. It was an enlightened, benign dictatorship he thought – but he couldn't argue with the results.

Tom finished his coffee and set off to find the yacht moorings and Devlin's boat; the *Kerkira*. Then he would visit the sailing club to see what he could find out about this man who was such a special friend of Miriam Maier.

It was an easy walk up through the hotel gardens and along the path which ran to the end of the island. Looking northwards, he could see how the stretch of flat water which ran between Tremorna and Cormoran, the nearest island, narrowed dramatically before entering the ocean and that the mouth of the channel was still guarded by the remains of two semi-ruined Martello Towers. The white surf of the open Atlantic smashed around them and reminded him that out there, beyond the headland, the shores of this place had been the rocky fate of many hundreds of ships in the eighteenth and nineteenth centuries and its crashing seas, the resting place of the thousands of souls who had sailed in them.

After about half-a-mile, the path steepened and as he rounded an outcrop of stone and heather, three large yachts came into view. They were moored about fifty-yards off shore, barely moving in the gentle swell and from the path, he could easily read the names on their bows – *Dawntreader*, *Cirrus Minor* and a brand-new 'Finngard-46' - *The Tilly*. There was no sign of life on the boats and no dinghies tied up alongside them. And there was no *Kerkira*.

He turned and headed back to the hotel, this time choosing to take the alternative route along the beach. It was a blissful walk in the sun, following the water's edge and thinking back to happy family holidays when the children were little, but he was tired and thirsty when he finally walked up the timber steps of the tiny sailing club to find a girl in her mid-twenties with tanned legs, sitting at a desk. She wore a long-sleeved, heavy cotton shirt, blue shorts and a pair of battered sailing shoes.

'Hello there – I'm staying up at the hotel,' he said, as he looked around the small hut. The place smelled of musty canvas and sea water.

'Would you like to hire a boat?' she said.

'Not today thanks. Do you look after the yacht moorings too?' he said.

'Yes - the rates are over there on that board. They're set according to size.'

'I'm really more interested in the boat *owners*. Have you worked here long?'

'Four years. I run the place,' said the girl.

'What a great way to earn a living…' he said, smiling at her, '…I'm envious, really.'

'If you're looking to buy a boat you've seen, leave me your contact details and I'll let the owner know…'

'The truth is,' he said interrupting her, 'I work for an insurance company. It's about a claim we're looking at. Someone died back in Polporth and we're still not sure about the circumstances which led to his death. I know you'll want to help.'

As he finished his sentence, her manner changed from polite helpfulness to nervous suspicion.

'I've a couple of questions to ask you but you'll want to be sure who I am first,' he said, smiling reassuringly as he passed her his ID and two printed emails. 'This is the phone number of the desk at Polporth police station. They'll tell you who I am.'

The girl looked carefully at Tom's identification and at the phone numbers of *Hendersons* and the Polporth police. 'Alright,' she said. 'Why don't you wait down by the water while I check these? Sorry, but...'

'Of course – just call out when you're done,' he said.

Ten minutes later, she beckoned him back up the steps into the clubhouse. She closed the door behind them and sat down at her desk.

'Before I talk to you, everything I say will be confidential - yes?' she asked. 'People come here to get away from it all and to let their hair down without anyone telling tales. I want to help but, well, you know.'

'Secrets are always safe with me,' he said as he sat down next to her. 'I'd like to see your mooring records; names, dates and times. Boats which either arrived or left in the last seven weeks. Particularly the bigger yachts.'

'That's easy enough,' she said, opening the pages of the ledger in front of her. 'It's all here.'

'There's not much to report. The French fifty-footer Eloise came at the beginning of July, then some Italians were here for three days in a catamaran on the 4th, the Kerkira left on the 8th, Tilly arrived on the 22nd and the lighthouse maintenance crew dropped by on the 23rd – they stayed for a cup of tea. Then Dawntreader and Cirrus moored up by the headland within a couple of days of each other last week. That's it.'

She sat back and looked at him, waiting for him to say something as he leant across and examined the pages of the register.

'Now I'm going to ask you about some people you may know,' he said. 'They may even be friends of yours, but this is important. I'm not going to ask you to point any fingers; you're just going to help me with some facts. Okay?'

She looked anxiously at him as if taken-aback by the formality of his tone but nodded.

'We know the Kerkira is owned by a Mr Patrick Devlin,' said Tom. 'Where did he say he was going to sail the boat the day it left? According to your records that would be Saturday the 8th.'

'He didn't take it anywhere – they went without him. They were taking the boat down to Greece for the rest of the summer.'

Tom frowned. 'Who are 'they'?' he said.

'Adrian and Ben,' she said. 'They're all friends. They stay on the boat together or up at the hotel. It's the two of them who are crewing the boat. Pat said he was going to fly out at the end of August so they could all bring the boat back. It's going to be his holiday I think.'

'Did you notice anything unusual going on before they left?'

'Not when they set-off, no. There wasn't much wind that morning so conditions weren't great for sailing but they seemed determined to get going. I suppose that's a bit odd but people do it sometimes.'

'Did you see Mr Devlin arrive here?'

'Yes, I was just opening up so it must have been about six-thirty - Pat had come straight here from the overnight ferry. He gave the boys a couple of holdalls – extra supplies for the trip I suppose, then they sailed-off.'

'Anything else?'

'Pat went up to the hotel to check-in for the weekend but they had a message for him. His friend, Anthony Maier, had died the night before but no-one had been able to contact him. The mobile phone coverage is patchy around Polporth and non-existent here. He flew straight back to the mainland on the afternoon plane. Georgia, the girl on the hotel reception desk told me.'

Tom looked at her for a few seconds, searching her face for any signs of a lie but all he saw was fear – she was afraid that she may have said things which could get someone into trouble.

'So he must have bought a standby seat on the plane. The computer didn't pick that up…' said Tom, muttering to himself.

'What computer?'

'It doesn't matter – one of our search engines needs tuning… I'm sorry - you've been very helpful Miss…?'

'I'm Sophie. Sophie Campbell. This is about Anthony Maier's death isn't it?'

'Yes, but don't tell anyone about me being here; it could compromise our enquiry,' he said, standing up. 'I'll be in the hotel – Room Twelve, if you need to call me.'

Tom Rohm thanked her again, said goodbye then spent the rest of the afternoon lying peacefully in the sun on the hotel terrace, reading again through the Anthony Maier case files. He was still looking for clues but if there was anything else in there, he couldn't see it.

That evening, he reluctantly decided to eat in the hotel dining room. He viewed the prospect with some misgivings because although he was comfortable as a lone traveller, he had found that eating by himself in restaurants could make for a self-conscious couple of hours, even with a good book or some work for company.

But still, he passed up the opportunity of room service, persuading himself that joining the other guests might offer the chance to discover more about Pat Devlin, perhaps courtesy of an overly talkative barman or a couple of hotel guests who might share some gossip after too much to drink.

As he drank his orange juice at the bar, he started a conversation with the thirty-something couple standing next to him. The three of them immediately hit-it-off and they asked him to join their party for dinner.

They were served by a well-dressed waiter with a good haircut and the atmosphere in the room with its Weeping Fig trees and softly-lit walls hung with limited edition prints was convivial.

His party consisted of the couple he had met at the bar - Harry and Chloe - whose young children were safely in bed, courtesy of hotel child care, plus Harry's sister and three other older couples whom, he was told, had been regular visitors to the hotel for years.

Harry told Tom that he worked for an investment bank, having been recruited straight from university after he finished his degree in History. He was a warm and entertaining man although his wife was altogether nervier; at times in the conversation, seeming to lose her self-confidence completely. Tom could see that she was an intelligent woman but was probably feeling the isolating effects of being marooned in the house after having the children. This was a real hazard for the modern, well-educated, stay-at-home mum, he thought to himself.

After the main course, Tom took his opportunity to casually mention that he knew Pat Devlin and wondered if anybody around the table had ever met him here at the hotel. Only Harry remembered him.

'Yes, I know the chap. I got introduced to him at the bar here a couple of years ago. He seemed the sort who feels a bit awkward in groups. He kept to himself...well, to himself with his two mates. They still come in here but usually sit by themselves. They seem nice enough, not exactly party animals though.'

After that, as it became clear that he wasn't going to learn much more about Devlin from anyone at the table, Tom decided to simply sit back and try to enjoy the rest of the night.

He felt exhausted and weather-beaten but two more hours passed quickly. The evening was drawing to a close when during a conversation with Harry about music, Tom let it slip that he could play the piano. Harry immediately saw the opportunity for some late night entertainment and the whole table was loudly informed. Of course, Tom *had* to play and they wouldn't take no for an answer.

After getting the go-ahead from the maître d', Tom walked across to the piano. He lifted the lid of the Blüthner baby grand, ensured that it was in tune with two arpeggios and then started to play a medley of Gershwin tunes, arranged for solo piano by the composer himself in 1932. In their day, they were regarded as popular entertainment pieces, but Gershwin had in fact used the arrangements as an opportunity to show-off his own dazzling virtuosity.

Tom's expressive musicality was such that even the most inebriated of the diners immediately quietened to a hushed whisper as his fingers danced over the keys and the notes cascaded out into the restaurant. He'd already played the up-tempo "Stairway to Paradise" when he segued effortlessly into "The Man I Love" before finishing with the poignant "Someone to Watch Over Me". He was only four bars into the Introduction of this final piece, when he realised too late what was happening to him. This had always been his favourite Gershwin song and it had been his wife's too. It had been playing at the party where they'd first met and it was the words to this song which she had playfully sung to him as they lay in bed after their first night together.

As he came into the bridge section, he didn't think he'd be able to keep going as everything he'd been through seemed to well-up and overwhelm him. Somehow he struggled through to the end as he looked down at the keyboard, hoping that no-one could see his face as he battled against the tide of emotion.

When he finished, there was a moment's silence before the whole restaurant burst into applause. He took a modest bow and returned to a hero's welcome at his table but stayed only briefly before making his apologies and leaving.

He swayed a little as he walked across the restaurant and out on to the moonlit terrace. Although it was now after eleven, the night was still hot and he felt faint from the effects of the afternoon sun. He looked out across the dark sea then bowed his head and wept. He cried for himself, for the lost love of his wife and for his children who'd never had the chance to get to know him as the father he could, and should, have been.

But it wasn't too late. He had turned a corner now. He had taken responsibility for the mistakes he'd made and had started to move on but now he realised this wasn't just about himself. He had to rebuild the trust of his children and of his old friends and remember again his need for other people and their need for him. He would have to learn again how to reach out and when he returned to Polporth, he would tell Tessa that for better or worse, he was falling for her. He would take that chance.

He went back to his room and lay on the bed thinking about the case. It was a dead end. They'd followed the company's protocols; he'd discharged his obligations and he felt good about himself. There was no more to be done.
Just before he turned in, he stepped out on to the terrace to breathe-in a final nightcap of the warm sea air. The night was clear but a fog warning could be heard coming from a lighthouse out on the westerly approaches to the islands. As he looked out towards the mouth of the channel, he could see the edge of a heavy sea mist rolling in. The weather was changing. Tomorrow he would return to the mainland and close the Anthony Maier case.

Chapter Fourteen

On the Beach

After she had dropped Tom off at the airport, Amelie had driven cautiously back to Polporth, taking care to maintain her nervous concentration on the hedge-lined bends of the narrow Cornish country roads. In spite of Tom's seemingly easy going attitude about the car, she knew that the tiniest blemish on the perfect body of the *Thetis* would be immediately noticed.

As she drove back down the hill into the town, she made a momentous decision - she was going to take the day off. There was no more to be done on the case and she persuaded herself that a break from her exam revision was much needed and well deserved. She made her plans quickly – there would be retail therapy, lunch and then the beach. The shopping was a success and it was just before one o'clock when she stumbled back into the Schooner Inn, tired and laden-down with bags of summer clothes, to find Detective Rob Tallis sitting there in the lobby. As soon as she came through the door he stood up.

'It looks like *you've* had a busy morning,' he said with a curl of a smile. 'I was passing so I dropped-in to see if you and Inspector Hound had finished your business yet.'

Amelie tried her best to appear un-fazed by his arrival but was sure she looked a mess and wouldn't know what to say to him. He helped her with her bags as she put them down, trying to regain her composure.

'I think you need some recovery time,' he said. 'Why don't you put this lot in your room and then we'll have a chat and cup of tea,' he said, pointing to the dining room. 'Do you need a helping hand?' he said, looking down at the shopping.

'No, its fine, I can manage,' she said.

But she couldn't manage. By the time she was halfway up the stairs, the bags had become snagged between the balusters and she found herself looking plaintively back down at him. He gave her an understanding nod then leapt into action.

'West Penwith police to the rescue Ma'am,' he said as he strode up the staircase to take the bags from her.

'It's number six,' she said.

'Got it,' he said as he made his way along the narrow hall before putting the shopping down outside her room. Then, after giving her a short, mock salute, he winked, turned and went back downstairs.

Five minutes later, with her hair brushed and skin perfumed, she was in the lobby and ready to go.

'All set?' he said. 'And where's your partner in crime?'

'Tom's away for a couple of days – some new information came in.'

'Information about what? Never mind, you can tell me all about it over coffee. Why don't we go round to the harbour? It's a beautiful day and it's better than sitting in here – this place feels like a bloody nursing home,' he said, making her giggle as they walked out through the front door.

On their way to the harbour, they passed the steps at the end of Love Lane. Amelie glanced along the row of cottages but Rob Tallis didn't even acknowledge their existence. Instead, he chatted away about how busy the police were at this time of year and how the influx of visitors always brought with it a wave of petty-crime which was difficult to get convictions on and impossible to prevent.

'They allocate resources based on the size of the population and the local crime rate across the whole year,' he explained, 'but we're seasonal here. Things are quiet between October and May but in the summer we just can't cope. My boss has a copy of a letter on his wall written by the Duke of Wellington saying he's fighting two wars – one against the French and another against his own civil service! Not much changes does it?'

When they reached the bottom of the hill, they turned and walked along the quayside towards a restaurant with bright yellow awnings and inviting tables set outside.

'It's almost one-thirty, do you feel like some lunch?' he said as they sat down. 'I think I'll have something, I'd lost track of the time.'

She was trying hard not to show it, but this was already feeling like fun.

'You're not in a rush?' she said, hoping he wasn't.

'Just for once, I'm not. I'd pretty much decided to take some time off this afternoon anyway - I'm owed enough. What do you fancy?' he said, looking down at the menu. She stole a suggestive glance across at him before seeing what the restaurant might offer.

And so they had lunch together. The wine, like the conversation, flowed easily and went quickly to her head. He had a wicked, flirtatious sense of humour and although she could see that the responsibilities of his job weighed him down, he was by nature someone who lived for the moment. Most of the men she had met in the last couple of years seemed, like her, to be deferring so much of themselves to their careers but Rob Tallis was a *now* person and she found herself liking him more and more. He was freer than she was. Then, just as they were just starting their coffee, he changed tack.

'I have to talk shop for a minute and then we can forget about it. What's new on the case and where has the Great Detective gone?'

'Tom's gone to the Karrack Islands to look into a couple of things. We don't know if it will lead anywhere.'

'You don't know if *what* will lead *where?*' he said, seeming mildly irritated. She wondered if they should have kept him better informed but given Tallis' previous lack of interest in what they were doing, she decided to hold the line. If this caused problems with the police, Tom could sort it out when he got back.

'You'll have to ask him. Sorry,' she said.

'And just where did this new information come from?' persisted Tallis.

'It's probably nothing. He didn't think it was worth discussing,' she said, trying hard to keep her nerve.

'Look, if you two don't want to involve us, that's your problem. I don't care as long as you don't cause trouble for anyone - particularly for me or my men.'

'It's not that I don't want to tell you, but I'd rather leave it for Tom to explain. I'm still very inexperienced you know,' she said looking into his eyes for some sign of sympathy. Rob Tallis gave her an understanding smile, shrugged, then leant forward, once more changing the mood of the conversation. 'Anyway, that's work isn't it and *we* could have a few hours off. It feels like skiving but do you fancy going to the beach? We could have a swim and a bit more of a natter.'

Without even thinking about it, she found herself saying 'yes'. The beach was what she was planning to do anyway, she told herself, so why not spend the afternoon with someone, rather than be alone. It was only when they were on the way back to the hotel to get her swimsuit that she wondered about the professionalism of it all. 'Just stay off anything to do with the case,' she reminded herself, 'then it would all be okay...'

Rob Tallis walked her back to the Schooner then went off to his flat to get changed; telling her that he only lived a mile away and would quickly come back to the hotel to pick her up.

Half-an-hour later, he arrived back in the lobby just as she came down the stairs dressed in her new shorts and T-shirt. He raised his eyebrows in pleasant surprise then nodded his approval.

The beach was busy but not so full that they weren't able to find a quiet corner in the sun. As they threw down their towels, he looked out at the ocean.

'Are you coming in?' he said, 'it'll be nice, I promise. The water's warm this time of year.'

As she pulled off her top and shorts to reveal her new bikini, he subtly watched her undress as if making careful mental notes about her barely clothed body – her smooth dark skin, her strong slim legs...

'Having just had you under careful surveillance, I'd have to report that you are in fact, *gorgeous*, just as I suspected,' he said.

She smiled shyly back at him.

'Come on,' he said, 'let's get into the water before the sight of you starts a riot. I'm meant to be off-duty.'

They were both strong swimmers and so powered-out confidently through the waves until they were clear of the surfers and the sea kayaks to where the water was flat. There they spent the best part of an hour, lying on their backs, treading water and talking about his life here in Cornwall and hers in London.

When the time came to swim back in and they were nearing the point where the surf began to break, he shouted over to her.

'Have you ever body-surfed?'

She shook her head.

'Well now's your chance,' he said. 'Take your time and wait for the right wave. Watch for them starting to build...out there,' he said pointing out to sea. 'Choose a big one, swim at the same speed then kick hard, stay on top and ride it in. Keep in front of the white water. Come on – we'll do it together.'

They held their position for a few minutes whilst Rob Tallis watched and waited before he pointed at a heavy, dark blue line, fifty-yards away, steadily increasing in size as it rolled in towards the beach. 'This one will do us,' he said.

As the wave got closer, he shouted more instructions across at her, 'ready, wait, wait, okay – start kicking...keep going...that's it!'

Sure enough, it worked. The huge breaker brought them into the shallows and up onto the sand.

'That was fantastic!' she said, still feeling the exhilaration of being carried so far, so fast, as they walked back up the beach.

'It's even better with a surf board,' he said laughing, '…but the principle's the same. It's all in the timing – about staying patient and spotting the opportunity. Then, when you think it's right, go for it. A bit like life.'

'And do you like your life here?' she said as they both stretched out on their towels.

'It's got its compensations…' he said lazily, '…days like this spent with beautiful girls from out of town.'

'What would your wife think of you saying things like that?'

'I don't have one; I'm divorced. No wife, no girlfriend just a couple of kids who live with their mother.'

He turned over onto his stomach, looking more thoughtful than before. 'No one wants to be with a low-paid copper working mad hours.'

'Oh I don't know…' she said, smiling at him.

He didn't respond immediately but then slowly lifted his head and looked straight at her.

'Thanks, but if you're trying to sell me insurance, I'm already covered,' he said as he lay his head back down again and closed his eyes, a faint smile remaining on his lips. 'Nice try though. If you keep it up, I might let you quote me.'

As they lay next to each other in the sun, surrounded by the familiar summer sounds of breaking waves and children's laughter, she opened her eyes and looked across at him. He had the strong build she would have expected in a man in his profession but to her surprise, she realised that being with him made her feel completely safe.

It was a new feeling for her and one that she realised had always been missing from her life. Was this the same warm sense of security that girls who'd grown up with caring fathers felt and so took for granted? And was this what being with a man who loved you was like? She didn't know; she was guessing. But she was hoping that it would feel as nice as this.

It was almost five o'clock when Rob Tallis looked at his watch and sat up.
'I've got to go. I'm picking the kids up from their grandmother's. Fancy a quick drink? We can drop-by my flat if you like, it's just up the hill,' he said, nodding in the direction of the end of the beach. 'Then I'll drive you back to the hotel on my way out of town.'
They got dressed and fifteen minutes later arrived at his sunny, tidy flat. Large windows in the small sitting room looked out over the beach and a set of double-doors led out on to a balcony with two silver café chairs and a round table. 'I sit out there and watch the sun set,' he said, '...when I get the chance that is, which isn't very often.'
He poured them both a glass of wine and they sat on the balcony, looking out across the sea and talking. After half-an-hour, Rob glanced at his watch. 'Sorry, but I really do have head-off,' he said reluctantly as he stood up. 'This has all been very nice, but duty calls.'
But as he went back inside, brushing against her as he passed by, she took his hand. Standing up, she pulled him slowly to her and spoke softly into his ear. 'Would we get into a lot of trouble...?'
'Only if we get caught,' he said with a smile. He looked again at his watch then shook his head. 'Well...I suppose the kids can wait for once.'

Chapter Fifteen

Changing Course

An hour later, Rob Tallis pulled-up outside the Schooner, kissed Amelie on the cheek and said goodbye.
'...and don't forget to tell Hercule Poirot to call me when he gets back.' Then he smiled, waved and accelerated away. Although she quickly dismissed the feeling, she didn't like the way they had parted by talking business. It had left the faintest of bitter tastes.

The next day, Tom's journey back to the mainland was difficult. The motor launch taking them from Tremorna to St Mawe had to navigate slowly through the sea fog which had rolled in overnight and his flight had been delayed for an hour. Finally, a break in the weather allowed them to take-off and once in the air, the clouds were left behind and the Cornish coastline quickly came into view.

Amelie was waiting at the airport to meet him and as they walked through the terminal building together and out into the car park, they talked about his trip.

'So how were the Karracks?' she asked as they approached the still pristine Thetis.

'I think I've finally found a hotel in England which I could recommend. Beautiful rooms looking out on empty, white beaches. I'd like to go back there one day.'

'Did you drink?' she said.

'No, I didn't. I know it looked bad before but I was never an alcoholic. I was someone who drank too much and there's a difference. It was what I was running away from which was the problem. You helped me exorcise that.'

'You may not have been an addict but it would have killed you if you'd carried on – you were dying inside Tom. Now, I'm happy for you.'

'Yes, I can see you are,' he said, noticing that something about her had changed. 'You look different. Is everything alright?'

'Everything's just fine. Rob Tallis came round. He wants you to call him. Anyway, what did you find out on the island?' she said, doing her best to appear calm and professional. But she felt neither calm nor professional after the events of the previous day and was sure that Tom could see it.

'Rob Tallis 'came round' did he? You must tell me all about it. We'll talk as you drive,' he said as he put his bags in the boot and ran a scrutinising eye over the bodywork of his car.

As they drove back to Polporth, he told her about Tremorna and the hotel, the walk along the coastline to find Devlin's boat gone, the sailing club and the conversation with Sophie Campbell.

'So what are you going to do now?' she asked.

He turned away and looked out of the car window at the flat countryside.

'Nothing. We sign-off the claim and go home.'

'You're not going after Devlin?'

'I've been thinking about it. There's no evidence a crime has been committed, certainly not one which would affect the claim. It's time to give up.'

'But we both know that something is going on here.'

'We *think* we do – that's not good enough.'

They drove on in silence for a few minutes before Amelie spoke very slowly, as if she was checking the logic of her own words as she went along.

'If there has been a crime and it's linked to Maier's death then it's *perfect* isn't it - the perfect crime is the one that goes undetected. We can see signs that something's happened but we don't know what.'

'And it'll stay like that,' said Tom. 'Crimes only get solved if the bad guys leave some evidence behind them and these people haven't. There's no trail to follow – all we've got is ripples on the surface of a lake.'

'So suppose we stir the waters?' she went on. 'What would happen if we make them think it *isn't* perfect; that we know something and we're coming after them?'

'They'll ignore anything we do.'

'Not if they're greedy.'

'A reward for information you mean?'

'It's our last roll of the dice.'

'Enson will be furious.'

'Best not to tell him then,' said Amelie.

At seven o'clock that evening, Tom got a call from Rob Tallis.

'I'm sorry you feel like that about it...okay...yes, we'll be here,' said Tom, ending the call and turning to Amelie. 'He's coming round here now – and he's not a happy policeman.'

A few minutes later, there was a loud knock on the bedroom door. Tom opened it to see a seething Rob Tallis holding a piece of paper which looked as if it had been torn from a wall somewhere.

"Robbery in Love Lane, Polporth; July 7th", said Tallis, reading from the flyer. "...our company is offering £10,000 for any information about this burglary. All calls will be treated in strict confidence... please call on 0799...' These are all over town and it's on the web too. Did you do this?'

'Come in, please,' said Rohm, ushering in the detective and closing the door. Rob Tallis barely glanced at Amelie before turning on Tom.

'What do you clowns think you're playing at? Every low-life and thief in the county will want a piece of it. Perhaps I didn't make myself clear – I told you to finish your business and go back to London.'

'There are some unanswered questions...' said Tom.

'Please don't say 'we think there's more to this than meets the eye,' interrupted Tallis.

'We do,' said Amelie.

Tallis rounded on her. 'Was I talking to you missy?' he said angrily. She rocked back, her mouth falling open as her eyes began to fill with tears.

'Don't speak to her like that,' said Tom looking the policeman straight between the eyes. Tom meant business and Tallis could see it.

'In my town, I'll speak to anyone any way I want,' said Tallis, leaning forward into Tom's face. For a few long seconds neither man flinched. Then Tallis blinked and stepped back.

'You're bloody fools,' he said. 'This'll end badly and I'm the one who'll have to clear up the mess.'

'Someone knows about that burglary and for ten-thousand, maybe they'll talk to us,' said Tom. 'It's possible Miriam and Devlin played a part in Maier's death - the break-in might be the key to it.'

'And suppose it isn't – suppose it was just kids or some local loser after a few quid for drugs?'

'Then end-of-story. We're out of here and on our way back up to London.'

'If we'd thought there was a connection between Maier's death and the burglary or the girl on Love Lane, we would have pursued it. There isn't so we didn't.'

'Did you know that Maier was having an affair and was probably going to leave his wife?' said Tom. 'That's motive.'

'For fucking what?' shouted Tallis, in exasperated frustration, looking as if he was about to start smashing the room up.

'That's what we're going to find out,' said Tom.

'*You're* going to find out are you - a pair of amateurs who're already way out of their depth?' He looked at them both, shook his head, turned and stormed out of the room, slamming the door behind him.

'We've really started something now haven't we?' said Amelie, still tearful.

Tom put a consoling arm around her shoulder and sat her down.

'Is there something you want to tell me?' said Tom.

'Only that I've been a fool.'

'Haven't we all - so now welcome to *my* club.'

Chapter Sixteen

An Inside Track

The next two days passed slowly. Each morning they would have breakfast together then read, rest, and take walks around the town whilst Tom patiently dealt with a steady stream of assorted lunatics and time wasters who would phone him to tell what they thought they knew about the burglary in Love Lane; which was nothing.
Tom had tried to call Tessa a couple of times and had even walked past the house but there was no sign of her.

It was just before eleven o'clock on the third morning after they had posted the reward when John Enson phoned. It was a call Tom had been expecting.
'What the hell is going on down there?' said Enson. 'I've just been speaking to a Detective Tallis - he's made a formal complaint. He told me you were in a fight and that you're being charged. He also said that you've offered a reward for information which has nothing to do with the claim and to cap it all, Pat Devlin told me yesterday that you went to High Cairn and upset Miriam. Have you gone *completely* mad?'

'I think there's a connection between a robbery and Maier's' death.'

'I didn't hire you to cause a fuss. No one wants this - the police don't want it, nor do the family or the Foundation and I certainly don't bloody want it. It's getting messy - finish this now or you're out.'

'Then I'm out. But I'll still file my report and you'll have to explain to the rest of the firm why you pulled the plug on an on-going investigation.'

Enson paused as if lost for words then continued on, calmer than before.

'You're a bloody fool who's chosen the wrong moment to try to prove that he isn't. Let me speak to Amelie.'

Tom passed the phone across to her then sat back, resigned to his fate. This was the end of the line for him, but he wasn't sorry. He'd tried his best and done what he thought was right. He had forgotten how good that felt.

'Yes, I do...' said Amelie, as she listened to what Enson was saying. 'No - I'm sorry. I can't do that Mr Enson...,' she said, '...yes...okay then. Goodbye.'

'Well?' said Tom.

'He wanted me to take over until he could find someone to come down here to sign-off the claim. I told him I wouldn't. Now we've got twenty-four hours to finish it or we're both fired. He says he'll do it himself if he has to.'

'Thank you,' said Tom.

'Have you got a spare bunk on that boat of yours?' she said nervously. 'I'm going to need a place to stay after my flat is re-possessed.'

He smiled at her.

'Are you lucky or unlucky?' he said.

'I used to think *lucky*.'

'Then we'll be fine. Just keep your nerve.'

Three hours later, Tom's phone rang again but this time the caller withheld their number. This time it was different.

'It's about your advert. I'd like to apply for the job,' said a man with a heavy local accent.

'And can I ask if you're properly qualified?' said Tom.

'If the money's right then I am. Ten grand is it? How do I know you'll pay?'

'If we're happy with your work, you'll be paid. We're London insurers and we get a lot of our work done this way. Information would soon dry-up if word got round that we didn't pay.'

'I'll do a good job and we'll set the record straight.'

'Where and when?'

'There's a pub called The Anchor. It's got a lane at the side of it that goes down to the water. I'll see you there at ten tonight. No one comes with you or I'm gone,' said the man and rang off.

'I think we have a deal,' said Tom.

Amelie looked anxiously back at him and held up a pair of crossed fingers.

At nine forty-five that evening, he put his jacket on and got up to leave.

'Are you sure not telling the police is a good idea?' said Amelie.

'They wouldn't let me do it and even if they did, they'd probably get spotted and frighten him off.'

'You're not doing this to prove something to us all are you?' she said.

'No, I'm proving something to me. This is the job - when it's done right. I'll be okay.'

Fifteen minutes later, Tom cautiously made his way down the unlit alleyway at the side of The Anchor pub. Just as the man on the phone had said, the sea was close-by and Tom could hear the sounds of waves crashing onto the beach at the end of the dark path. Half-way along, standing in the shadows of a doorway, he could see a man smoking a cigarette. Tom walked up to him and stood still as the man leant forward and looked back along the alleyway, checking to see that they were alone.

'So what have you got for me?' said Tom in a quiet voice.

'Where's the money?' said the man.

'If I'm happy, we'll set up the pay-off at a place you choose. I don't carry ten grand around in my pocket. You'll get paid next week.'

'I fucking better,' said the man edgily before he drew hard on his cigarette.

Tom frowned to himself. Why the big deal he wondered? Perhaps the break-in at Love Lane was more than just a small-time burglary worth a few hundred pounds. This man was really afraid.

'Someone's said something haven't they?' said the man. 'You think we topped him – that's why you put out the reward. Well we didn't – you get that straight,' he said, putting out his cigarette and immediately lighting up another.

'It should have been a quick in and out job. We had a shopping list. The statue wasn't there but we got the rest of it. Then we're leaving when this old bloke walks around the corner and sees us coming out...'

Laughter echoed between the buildings as two men walked past the end of the alley way and went inside the pub. The man in the doorway stood in silence for few seconds, listening. When he was sure they were still alone, he continued his story.

'The stupid bastard starts shouting for us to stop so I go back up the lane to shut him up. There's a bit of pushing and shoving then he holds his chest. But that was it - I didn't hit him, he just went down.'

Tom looked sceptically back at him.

'Look - he was alive when we left him. Whatever happened after that wasn't my fault. I don't want no big insurance company and the London police coming after us.'

'So you left him outside Number Four?'

'We had to run for it. He must have crawled off looking for help and then nose-dived down those steps.'

'And what did you do after you left him there?' said Tom.

'We drove out of town, dropped the stuff off and picked up our money - at the old mine at Pendean. That's it.'

'Who gave you the shopping list?'

'Oh no - that's not for sale.'

'I need the name of the person who set this up. Maybe it was someone you owed a favour to? The police will understand.'

'You don't want to know mate, trust me - you'll be safer. It was a little blag that went wrong that's all. Now about my money...'

'Half the story only gets you half the money.'

'You bastard.'

'Give me a call in a week and the firm will be ready to pay you.'

The man looked nervously along the alleyway then turned to Tom. 'I shouldn't have come here. You just remember what I told you. Him dying wasn't our fault,' he said. Then he turned up his collar and hurried away.

Tom gave him a minute then walked back up on to the street to return to the Schooner. He got out his phone and called Amelie.

'Hi – I'm okay. I think I know…'
But before he could say anymore, something hit him hard on the back of the head. He went down, his mind reeling and his focus gone. He was dimly aware of someone stamping on his phone before they dragged him down a set of steps and along a rough path. A door was kicked open and he felt himself being pulled across the stone floor of what smelt like a damp storeroom.
Lying semi-conscious in the darkness, he heard the sound of an iron drain cover being lifted off and then the swirl of rushing water echoing up from sewer pipes far below.
As he was being hauled across the floor towards the open drain, Tom let out a groan and urged his muscles back into action. He reached out, grabbed hold of the base of a timber post then braced himself for the inevitable pain as his attacker swung round and began to kick at his arms, trying to force him to let go. Then, just as he began to lose his grip, Tom heard a woman's voice shout out. It was Amelie.
'I've found him…he's in here,' she said.
The attacker stopped kicking, stood still, then was gone. Seconds later, the door to the storeroom slowly opened and the beam of a flashlight swept across the floor. Amelie rushed over to him and after pushing his hair back off his bleeding face, took out her phone and called the police.

An hour later, a now conscious but bruised and bloody Tom Rohm lay in his bed in the Accident and Emergency ward, looking up at Amelie and Rob Tallis as they stood over him.

'If something bad happens once, it's unlucky. If it happens twice, it looks like a habit. You must enjoy getting beaten up,' said a grouchy Tallis. 'The bloke who hit you was probably one of the informer's mates who thought you had the money on you. I bloody warned you didn't I? I told you this would end in trouble.'

'I'm beginning to see Polporth in a whole new light – this is a rough town,' said Tom. Then he turned to look up at a concerned Amelie. 'You called out to make him think the police were with you. Thanks.'

'I'll be heading off now,' said Tallis, unimpressed, as he put away his notebook. 'When you're up to it, drop by the station, sign a statement then this time, leave town. Until you do, try to stay out of trouble.'

'"Trouble just follows me around." It's from an old blues song,' said Rohm. Tallis shook his head and walked out of the cubicle, irritably pulling the curtain across behind him.

'How did you get there so quickly?' said Tom, turning to Amelie.

'I was around the corner from the pub the whole time,' she said.

'Did you see the man who hit me?'

'I was too far back. But I heard you go down then followed the sound. You're one lucky Claims Man.'

'I'm a Claims Man who's lucky to have you.'

'Rest now – I'll be back in the morning to take you to the hotel,' she said running a soothing hand across his forehead. But instead of lying back, Tom raised himself up on one elbow, beckoning her to him so he could whisper into her ear.

'I told Tallis I didn't remember what happened after I was hit, but I do. The man who attacked me wasn't trying to rob me; he was trying to kill me. You saw that open shaft in the storeroom? It's part of the town's drainage system I think – it runs out under the sea. He was going to throw me down it.'

Amelie stood slowly back with a look of horror on her face. Tom nodded at her.

'What have we got ourselves into here?' she said.

'I believed our Burglar Bill – someone else was behind the robbery in Love Lane. They'll all be facing manslaughter charges but that's for another day. Right now, I need to get some answers.'

He got out of bed, waving away her attempts to help him up.

'Go back to the hotel and this time wait there,' said Tom, stretching and holding his bruised and aching back. 'Can I use your phone? – I need to tell someone I'm coming round to finish a little game of kiss and tell.'

'You're mad – you can hardly stand up,' she said.

'I'm tougher than I look. Now if you don't mind, I'm going to get dressed,' he said. It was clear that this wasn't a matter for negotiation.

It was just after midnight when Tom Rohm walked stiffly up the steps of Number 4 Love Lane, knocked and waited. As soon as the door was opened he pushed inside and closed it quickly behind him.

Tessa Varle stepped back, shocked by his appearance.

'My God, what happened?' she said, clutching the front of her gown.

'Why don't *you* tell me?'

'I've been here all evening - how would I know...?'

'Not tonight - I know what happened tonight and it was quite a lot as you can see. Tell me about the break-in and why Anthony Maier was on Love Lane the night he died.'

'I don't know why he was here...I've told you before. You should sit down. I'll make some tea,' she said, starting to walk towards to kitchen.

'I don't want any bloody tea - I want you to tell me everything. Tell me about artists and stolen sculptures - and don't bother with the 'little girl lost' routine.'

She looked at him; frightened, as if unsure what he would do next.

'Someone tried to kill me tonight Tessa. Now why would they want to do that?'

'Oh Tom...' she said, starting to weep. 'I'm so sorry. I thought the police would catch the men who broke-in and bring her back to me. But now this has happened...I think *they've* got her. They'll do anything to keep her.'

'They?'

'Miriam and Devlin.'

'Why would they want it - what's so special about that sculpture?'

She stood weeping, her face buried in her hands.

'Tessa, if you don't tell me, we're going down to the police station.'

'Alright...,' she said, looking up at him with tears running down her face.

'That little sculpture – the figure of the girl; it's you isn't it? Is that what this whole thing's been about?' asked Tom.

'She was a study for a life-sized piece which Anton did for St Cecilia's College in Oxford...it's in their garden. It's called *Love*. Anton never really liked it.'

'I remember it,' said Tom. '...it was in a book about his work.'

'But did your book say that mine was called *Desire* and the best thing he ever did? She was only shown once in a gallery and everyone loved her. Then he gave her to me.'

146

'So it's worth a fortune?'

'Anton thought perhaps five-million pounds. She was my rainy day money he said; in case I was left alone.'

'But why didn't you keep it safe - in a bank or a vault somewhere?'

'You don't lock your children away do you? You have them with you out in the world. And I could never have sold her...she was like our daughter you see. We made her together.'

'Why didn't you tell the police what it was?'

'I thought the safest way of getting her back was if no-one knew who she was or what she was worth. I hoped the break-in was just some locals and we'd find her in an antique shop somewhere.'

'How old were you when you posed for him?'

'Fifteen. And to save you the embarrassment of asking; yes - we did.'

'And it carried on?'

'After my mother died, he helped me buy this house so we could be together. He said that one day, he would leave Miriam and marry me,' she said as if it had all been some sad, hopeless dream.

'Do you know the history of these houses Tom? This was where the town prostitutes lived - for the sailors. *Love Lane* you see. No windows on to the street - just dark rooms for guilty secrets. We could be together here, hiding and ashamed.'

'Did Miriam know about you?'

'Not at the beginning – but later, yes.'

'And about the sculpture?'

'Yes. And she hated us for it.'

Tom stood silently for few seconds, trying to process the tragedy of her story.

147

'Why did he come here the night he died? You were in Dartington weren't you?'

'I don't know. I think he may have forgotten I was away. He'd just come back from America.'

'So he shouldn't have even been here. It was just bad luck.'

'We were never meant to be happy. Perhaps we were cursed by the spirits of the women who used to live in these houses.'

'I think he came here to tell you something important; something which couldn't wait. He was going to leave Miriam - to be with you. Ashley told me.'

'Yes…to be with me…' she said slowly. It was as if the thought of how close she had come to finally being with the man she loved was too much to bear and she had gone into a place where there was no more pain.

'I have to leave,' said Tom. 'I've got to finish this now.'

'Please stay,' she said, moving closer to him and touching his face. She kissed him as she slowly pulled the robe off her shoulders and let it fall to the floor.

He looked at her pale, naked body and then watched her close her eyes as she shaped his fingers, moving his hand slowly downwards. As she pulled him closer, her body beginning to arch back as she responded to his touch, she whispered something to him; not clearly at first but then unmistakably,

'Darling…Anton…you've come back to me.'

He froze, gently pushing her away from him as he looked into her face. Her eyes were still closed, lips parted as if awaiting the kiss of her dead lover. Now he knew she could never be his. She was in love with a ghost and they would belong to each other forever.

'I'm sorry Tessa. If you ever need me, just call, but now I have to go,' he said softly, as he picked up her robe and draped it back around her shoulders. She stood looking at him as if she was still in her dream, smiling like a lost child as he closed the door and walked away.

Chapter Seventeen

When the Birds Have Flown

Amelie came down to breakfast to find a pale and exhausted-looking Tom Rohm sitting at a table drinking a large cup of black coffee. His laptop was switched on, the case files were out and there were pages of scribbled notes in front of him.

'You remember the picture of Tessa outside of the gallery? Well this is her too,' he said, passing Amelie the photograph of *Desire* then sitting back in his chair, his hands clasped behind his head.

'That sculpture was in Tessa's house and its worth millions. Maier gave it to her because they were a couple. She was the one he was going to leave his wife for.'

'Did Miriam know?'

'I think she knew it all.'

'So she set up the break-in to take it - to get back at Maier and Tessa?'

'Except that Burglar Bill said the statue wasn't there. I believed him then and I still do.'

'And you're sure Tessa told you the truth – that she told you everything?'

'No, I'm not sure at all. She told me once that she sits by that chapel above the town every day and looks out at the sea. She's been doing it for years I think, whenever Maier was away. It was as if she was waiting for him – the sailor home from the sea. Then, when he finally returns, this time to stay, he goes and dies on her. I think she may have gone a bit mad.'

'But if Tessa and the thief are *both* telling the truth…?' said Amelie, looking confused.

'Then someone else must have gone in and taken the sculpture between Tessa going away and the break-in five days later.'

'If the alarm is only set-off on the night of the robbery - whoever came in had a door key *and* knew how to disarm the system.'

'The key isn't so much of a problem - pay a dodgy locksmith to get you something which will work, or acquire a copy of the original somehow. It's the alarm that's the puzzle - it's impossible to beat. Maier had it put it in to protect his masterpiece. But look at this…'

Tom leant forward, typed on to his laptop then turned the screen around so that Amelie could see one of the technical manuals which he had on his hard disk.

'Tessa's alarm system is the *Packart Vista 120X*,' he said. 'When I tested it that first time, the control box went through some strange sequences then shut-down completely before re-booting itself. So I've just told the trouble-shooting programme here what happened and asked it to *diagnose*…' he said, hitting the 'enter' key. They both looked at the screen as the bright blue text came up in short bullet points alongside the circuit codes for each part of the system being scrutinised.

'This is telling me it behaves like that when someone has overridden the alarm using the manufacturers' security codes.'

'And who would have access to those?'

'No-one apart from the programmers themselves and the systems guys who install them.'

'How many of them are there?'

'For an advanced programme like this - only two or three people in the whole country.'

'Could Devlin or Miriam have got to one of them?'

'Normally I'd say 'no'. They're pretty much incorruptible but for Miriam Maier, money is no object so maybe that's a 'yes'.

'So she and Devlin could have gone in themselves, taken the statue then hired the thieves to make it look like an ordinary burglary. Tessa and Anton would never have suspected what had really happened.'

'I think we've got a few more questions for those two. Why don't we drop-by and surprise them,' said Tom.

An hour later, they arrived at High Cairn to find the gates open and with no response from the gate phone, drove in, parked and walked up to the front door of the house. No-one answered when they knocked and so they walked back up the drive to see if anyone was at home in the flat above the garage. What they found was an open front door.

'Hello?...' shouted Tom. They went cautiously up the stairs and into the silent flat, going first to the kitchen and then to a darkened bedroom to find Nina Choi, Miriam's Chinese housekeeper, lying on a bed, surrounded by lit candles and photographs of what Tom took to be the Maier children.

Seeing an empty bottle of whisky and a box of pills beside the bed, he rushed forward to check for vital signs. She was still alive.

'They've gone,' said Nina in a weak voice. 'Mrs Maier... left... gone to the house in Greece – she's going to sell here and I'll have nowhere to go. I looked after Mr Anton and the children and now nothing left...after all the years...'

'Everything will be okay,' said Tom, gesturing to Amelie to call for an ambulance.

'They went last night. Now I have to leave and Mr Anton is gone. He was a so special man.'

Fifteen minutes later, Tom and Amelie stood outside the flat, watching as the paramedics stretchered the recovering patient into the back of the ambulance.

'She'll be alright,' said Tom.

'She will, but what about us? What do we do now?'

'What do you do when the birds have flown?'

'Fly after them of course.'

'Are you sure you want to?' said Tom. 'We'll have to do it on our own - Enson won't pay.'

'I have some money.'

He nodded at her. It was no more than he had come to expect.

'Don't tell anyone what we're doing. We'll get the address of Miriam's house in Greece from the firm's database but as far as *Hendersons* and the police are concerned, the case is closed and we're going back up to London. We don't trust anyone until this is over.'

She nodded then smiled at him.

'We better get going then,' she said. He put his arm around her shoulder and gave her a reassuring hug.

'About Rob Tallis…' she said as they walked back to the car. 'I know I gave you a hard time about Tessa but I crossed a line too. I think you should know about it.'

'I'd already guessed. He's a good-looking man.'

'He's a particular sort of charmer - the sort that's hard to resist,' she said.

Then she told him how Tallis had come to the hotel, about their lunch together, the afternoon on the beach and what happened when they went back to his flat. Tom was silent as she recounted her story.

'That's why I was so upset when he turned on me. He was like a different person - it was as if we had never happened. He has a scary side.'

'Yes, I saw it too,' said Tom.

Chapter Eighteen

Under the Cypress Trees

As the Ionian coast came into view through the aeroplane window, Tom Rohm smiled to himself. This was the scene of Odysseus' homecoming and as the jagged shores drew closer, it seemed to him that he too had been on a journey home. He had crossed dark lands and angry seas and had, for a time, been bewitched by the siren voices of bitter-sweet melancholy, beckoning him on to the rocks of self-destruction. He had survived, so far, but Odysseus had returned to find that there were still more battles to be fought and Tom wondered what further trials awaited him before he could finally reclaim his selfhood.

After a bumpy landing buffeted by the capricious cross-winds for which the small airport was well known, they stepped out from the aircraft on to shaky steel steps and into what felt like a wall of heat. Looking out over the roofs of the terminal buildings, they could see small white houses set amongst densely planted olive groves, marching up the surrounding hillsides. In the distance, the island's main town shimmered in the heat haze, the ochre-coloured Herculean masonry of its defensive walls standing resolutely against the deep Mediterranean blue of the sea.

They collected their luggage and then along with the other jostling arrivals, made their way out to the taxi-ranks and the smells of *tiropita*, tobacco smoke and pine trees in hot summer air.

An hour later they had checked into their no-star hotel and hired a cheap car from a chain smoking, unshaven man who spoke little English. It was late afternoon by the time they drove out of town to find Miriam Maier's villa.

A wide, gently curving country road with trees on both sides, climbed up into the hills which ran like a protruding spine along the entire length of the island. As they went higher, pale yellow rocks and shale claimed the landscape and as the road narrowed and began to wind more sharply, the steel Armco barriers became more frequent.

After twenty minutes, they turned off the main highway and descended down towards the coast, coming eventually to a small town set amongst fertile fields. The place consisted entirely of vernacular buildings with stuccoed walls and terracotta roofs and as they drove along its main street, they attracted the stares of the old men who sat at the tavernas with their Ouzo and *komboloi*.

A mile out of town, they turned down an unmade road before stopping outside an imposing three-storey, neo-classical house. As the billowing cloud of white road dust slowly cleared, Tom and Amelie got out of the car, walked through the open gates of the driveway and around to the rear of the house.

Three Mercedes Benz cars stood parked under a row of tall cypress trees next to wide stone steps which led up to a mosaic-tiled terrace and an ornate door of red-brown varnished hardwood. Rohm walked up to it then stood for a moment, gathering his thoughts.

At first, all was quiet with only the sound of the *cicadas* filling the still air but then, as he was about to knock, he heard laughter echoing round from the side of the house. He said nothing but gestured to Amelie to follow him as he walked slowly back down the steps and across to another terrace which ran up to a low wall with an iron gate in it. The closer they came to the wall, the more they could see of a bright-blue swimming pool with two young men floating on their backs in the water, speaking in English. Tom didn't recognise either of them and was about to apologise for his intrusion when he saw someone he did know. Sitting on a chair by the side of the pool with an open book on his lap was Pat Devlin.

As soon as he saw Tom, Devlin stood up and called out. 'Miriam. We've got visitors.'

Seconds later, Miriam Maier emerged from the house wearing a swimsuit and holding what looked like a large cocktail. She stared at Tom in a way which told him she was neither pleased nor angry – just surprised. No one said anything.

Tom was about to speak when he heard another man's voice coming from the room behind her.

'Who is it...?' said the man as he walked out into the sun. It was John Enson.

Now it was Tom's turn to look surprised.

'Well, well...' said Enson, looking at Tom. 'At least you're not causing trouble in Cornwall. What the devil are you doing here?'

'I might ask you the same thing John?'

'I'm on holiday,' said Enson, as if it was the most natural thing in the world.

'With the wife and kids?' said Tom as he opened the gate and walked down to the side of the pool.

'As a matter of fact, no. They're back in England. What do you want?'

'We're dying to tell you all about it. Shall we go inside?' said Tom, his mind racing as he tried to run through the possible reasons why Enson would be here now, of all times.

'I suppose we should. It's alright,' said Enson turning to Miriam, 'they won't be staying long.'

Tom and Amelie followed Enson, Devlin and Miriam into the country kitchen and everyone sat down at the large rectangular table in the centre of the room. Tom studied both men's faces before turning to Miriam.

'Your husband died after struggling with thieves who broke into a house on Love Lane. Thieves who were sent there to steal *Desire* - the sculpture he gave to Tessa Varle,' said Tom.

'Thieves killed Anton? What is he talking about?' said a confused Miriam as she looked first at Enson and then across at Devlin.

'What has Miss Tessa Varle been saying?' said Devlin jumping to his feet.

'Why did you go to the trouble of stealing the statue before the burglars could get it Mr Devlin? Did you think they might have taken it for themselves?' said Tom, coolly blocking Devlin's outburst with a raised hand. 'You had it taken from Love Lane then put on your boat and brought here. Have you given Miriam your prize yet?'

'What prize? Are you mad? I've never...' Devlin stopped in mid-sentence; his expression suddenly changing as if he'd had a terrible realisation. He looked across at Enson, staring at him in wide-eyed shock.

'I don't think now is the right time...' said Enson, his eyes darting nervously between Miriam and Devlin.

'I know that look John, you're hiding something,' she said. 'Tell me what happened.'

Enson moved uncomfortably in his seat then took a deep breath.

'Pat brought the thing here on his boat without realising what it was,' he said, looking at the floor. 'I gave it to him – I told him it was a piece of art for the house – a surprise, for you.'

'Yes, it was heavy,' said Devlin.

'That's right Pat. It was a heavy burden. I'm sorry I deceived you.'

'What have you done?' said Miriam, as she glared at Enson in disbelief, her hand over her mouth.

'Don't look at me like that,' said Enson. 'Anton was going to leave you for that slut...'

Tom looked at Enson – amazed at what he was only now beginning to comprehend.

'It was you all along. You were behind the whole thing.'

'He was leaving you,' said Enson, still staring at Miriam as he implored her to understand.

'But he never got the chance did he?' said Tom. 'He died on Love Lane after a run-in with your hired help.'

'That was never meant to happen. How the hell was I to know he'd walk in on it? The bloody fool must have chased after them and then his heart gave out...' said Enson, turning to look at Miriam. 'It was my gift to you. I couldn't stand to see it eating you away - Anton, Tessa and that damned statue. Everyone said it was the best thing he ever did and it wasn't yours.'

'Is it here in this house?' said Miriam.

'Yes. She was their child but now she belongs to you.'

'I don't want it John. And I don't want you. You killed my darling Anton.'

'It was an accident…it was always me who loved you. He never cared for you the way I do…no one could.'
'I loved Anton. No matter what he did, I never stopped loving him,' she said.

Miriam buried her face in her hands and wept as John Enson looked down, his world lying like a broken mirror in pieces around him.
'We're going to take you and the sculpture back to London,' said Tom, looking at Enson. 'We can wait until we get home before the police get involved or I can call-in the Greek cops now. Best to come quietly back to England with us I think – it'll be less upsetting for your friends here.'
'Do whatever you want. None of it matters.'

Tom looked closely into John Enson's face as if still trying to fathom exactly what had happened. 'I really am very impressed John - it was brilliant. It had to look like a routine break-in so that Anthony Maier wouldn't suspect anything but you wouldn't have trusted local crooks with five-million pounds worth of art so you got there before them.'
'I'll talk to the police but I'm not talking to you,' said Enson, looking up at Tom.
'It would have been easy to copy the door key – Maier trusted you and you were often in his house,' continued Tom. 'You knew about the alarm but you had access to the manufacturer's codes to override the sequencing. Gerry Eames at *Hendersons* told me you designed the new office security set-up yourself. Did you choose the same systems so you could get the codes?'
Enson said nothing as he stared contemptuously back at Tom.

'After a few months, you'd say you traced the statue through the firm's connections with the stolen art recovery agents and then bring it to Miriam as a token of your love. She could keep it and Anthony would be none the wiser - he'd be with Tessa and believe it was still lost.'

'You think you're so bloody clever don't you…' said Enson.

'Him dying like that could have been a game changer but you kept your nerve,' said Tom. 'You knew if you worked it right you could still win – you would get Miriam *and* keep the sculpture. You'd have the chance of a good life with her here, away from the memory of her dead husband.'

Enson stood up as he started to lose control but Tom continued on.

'There was just one last item on your to-do list - get the Life Assurance claim settled so that everything looks normal. That's where I came in wasn't it? Get that drunken deadbeat Tom Rohm to do a crap job. He won't ask too many questions; he'll just sign it off, pick up his fee and everyone's happy…'

Enson lunged across the table but Tom was too quick and wrestled him to the floor, holding him face down in an arm lock.

'Tom – don't!' shouted Amelie jumping to her feet.

'You set me up,' said Tom, as he looked down at his broken enemy.

'I'd done it before,' said Enson. 'Why not again?'

'What's that?'

'That Reuters Claim of yours ending in tears…Jackson and the case files disappearing – all my own work. You could have got in my way for promotion to the Board and I never liked you much anyway. It was like mixing business with pleasure,' said Enson.

'Tom...let him go now,' said Amelie, edging warily towards the two men, fearing Tom might kill his man there and then.

'It's all right. Everything's under control. I wouldn't want this bastard to miss his day in court...'

Chapter Nineteen

Loose Ends

'So how are you feeling now, 'champ'?' said Amelie as she sat down next to Tom in the hotel bar. 'Job done - case closed. Tomorrow we take Enson and the statue home and you're a hero.'

'Not quite,' said Tom as he looked thoughtfully at the grenadine in his orange juice as it spiralled downwards in the glass. 'I always felt there was something odd about Maier dying the way he did and I've just worked out what it was. What did Enson say? "The bloody fool must have chased after them…" Even you thought that it might have happened like that - Maier pursues them then has a coronary and falls down the steps. Do you remember - you suggested it to Tallis?'

'At that first meeting at the police station, it seemed like a possible explanation.'

'If we believe the robber's account, there's some pushing and shoving then after Maier collapses, they leave him in front of Tessa's house and run off. So why doesn't Maier call 999 on his mobile phone - the police found one in his pocket? Instead, he staggers to the top of a set of steps which are so steep you could abseil down them. But he doesn't sit down to rest or make that call; he topples head first down the bloody lot and dies.'

'And why couldn't that have happened?'

'Because if you're having a heart attack, you don't chase anybody anywhere - you don't even wander off looking for help. I remember reading that it hurts like hell; like a barrel vice around your chest. You don't move. So how did he get from Number Four to the top of those steps? It's thirty-feet away.'

'Someone helped him...' said Amelie, 'but who would have wanted to do that?'

'Let's suppose Enson asked someone else to set this up for him. He tells them that the statue is worth say, a hundred thousand and that he'll pay him half that to steal it.'

'But they don't tell the robbers the true value?'

'No – that would be too much of a temptation. The burglars think it's only worth a few hundred because that's all they're getting paid. On the night of the robbery, this someone is watching from the shadows just to make sure things go according to plan. When the thieves come out of Tessa's house, our someone thinks they've got the statue but then Maier stumbles into it. He challenges them, sees their faces and they struggle - then he collapses.'

'And now our man has a problem – his hirelings can be identified and through them, so can he. He has to act fast.'

'So he watches the robbers run off then he goes to Maier, helps him up, dusts him off and walks him along the lane. He tells him everything is going to be alright. He says that the ambulance will come soon and that they need to get to the end of the street. They get to the top of the steps and stand there for a few seconds. Then he gives Maier a gentle push...and it's all over.'

'And it looks like a heart attack followed by a fall?'

'Natural Causes – with a helping hand.'

'If there was someone else involved, then our Mr Enson has been holding out on us.'

'And what he doesn't realise is that if we're right, then this someone is a very dangerous man and he'll be coming after him next. I think we should let him know, don't you?'

An hour later they stood outside Miriam's house as the front door was opened by one of Devlin's young friends. 'What do you want now?' he said. 'Haven't you done enough damage for one day?'

'I'm sorry,' said Tom, not really meaning it, 'but I have to see Mr Enson. It's very important.'

The man grudgingly opened the door and gestured for them to come inside.

'I'll get him,' he said, then disappeared down the hall.

Thirty seconds later, Enson emerged looking very much the worse for wear. He'd been weeping and was holding a glass of wine as he walked slowly towards them.

'You better come in here,' he said, leading them into a large sitting room.

Enson slumped down on to a sofa and sipped his wine.

'Well? Have you come to gloat?' he said.

'We've got some loose ends to tie-up John.'

Enson looked straight ahead and stayed silent.

'If you don't play ball, we'll have to involve Miriam and your friends here. They're all accessories to manslaughter and part of a conspiracy - they'll be charged alongside you.'

'But they had nothing to do with any of it. You know that,' said Enson, leaning drunkenly forward and glaring at Tom.

'We'd let the court decide who knew what.'

'You bloody bastard, you would too.'

'So now that I have your full attention…' said Tom.

Enson sat back resentfully and waited for the questions to begin.

'Can you describe the men you hired to take the statue?'

'I can't remember them – we only met once.'

'Where?'

'In a pub in Polporth'

'Which one?'

'I don't recall. Why does it matter?'

'And the date?'

Enson took another gulp of wine but said nothing.

'Last chance John and then we're gone. Your friends will face the music standing next to you in court.'

Enson looked away.

'You can't describe the robbers because you never met them,' said Tom. 'Someone else hired them for you and planned the break-in. Who was it - someone you knew through the firm's dubious but necessary connections with London criminals? Did you say the statue was worth a lot of money and you'd give him half? What did he end up with when it wasn't there?'

'I…I can't tell you anything,' said Enson.

'Why are you protecting him? You're scared of him aren't you? You should be,' said Tom.

Enson looked up at him.

'Anyone having a heart attack wouldn't stagger thirty-feet to fall down a set of steps - someone helped Maier on his way because he'd seen the robbers' faces. The night I met one of thieves, the same man tried to kill me because I was getting close to the truth.'

Enson look back down at the floor but still said nothing.

'He'll come after you now John. He'll come after all of you – poor old Pat and his boyfriends and Miriam too. Now, what did you tell him had happened to the statue?'

Enson looked nervously at Tom then took another large mouthful of wine.

'Okay – we're going,' said Tom. 'You had your chance so don't say I didn't warn you...'

'I told him Tessa Varle must have moved it,' said Enson, his fear of what might happen finally causing his resistance to buckle.

'I said that I was as surprised as he was when it wasn't there and that I'd find out what had happened. I gave him ten-thousand on account.'

'He won't be happy with that – not now,' said Rohm. 'He'll put the squeeze on you because you're implicated in a murder. He hasn't told you that yet, but he will.'

Enson stared at Tom as the horror of what might be coming his way hit home.

'And he may even be thinking you cheated him up over the statue,' said Tom, 'that it's worth a fortune but that you lied. He doesn't trust anyone now and he can see the chance of a big pay-off.'

'Oh Christ...' said Enson. 'Miriam could get hurt.'

Rohm sat down and picked up Enson's glass of wine. He raised it up to his mouth, closed his eyes and rotated the glass gently in his hand as the bouquet drifted upwards.

'He can smell big money John. It's so close, he can almost taste it,' he said as he put the glass back down on the table. 'So here's what we're going to do...'

Chapter Twenty

A Meeting of Minds

At ten o'clock the next morning, Tom and Amelie were back in Miriam's house looking at John Enson as he sat opposite them on the sofa. Out in the hall, a line of suitcases stood next to a small crate covered with 'Handle With Care' labels. They were all on their way home.

'Okay John – make the call,' said Tom, 'and put it on *speaker.*'
Enson picked up his phone and dialled.
'Yes?' said a man on the other end.
'I've got it,' said Enson. There was silence. The seconds seemed to be double their normal length as Tom and Amelie both held their breath and waited. Then the man spoke again.
'Where was it?'
'In Maier's studio, up at his house. He must have moved it there. The girl probably saw those two clods you hired hanging around Love Lane and they got nervous.'
'So you'll get a buyer?'

'I don't want any more to do with it. It's yours – sell it for what you can. It's cost us all too much already. I'm finished.'

'Suit yourself.'

'It'll be at the mine at eleven tomorrow night.'

'It's been nice doing business with you again.'

'I only wish I could say the same,' said Enson and rang off.

'Very good John,' said Tom. 'Most heartfelt – I almost believed you myself. But then you always did find it easy to fool me. It's time to go.'

The flight home was uneventful and the unceremonious handing-over of Enson to the police at London airport, swift and matter-of-fact. Tom and Amelie went to his houseboat, picked up the car and drove to Cornwall as fast as the old girl could carry them. By eleven o'clock that night, they were sitting in the *Thetis*, looking out at the tall chimney of the old Pendean mine, standing black against the moonlit sky.

'I still can't believe it. He was just using me to find out if you knew anything. To be that close to someone and not even suspect them...' said Amelie.

'Yes you did,' said Tom. 'After that scene at the Schooner when he lost it, you could see he had another side.'

'I saw something dark, but nothing like this.'

'He's a lying, manipulative psychopath so don't beat yourself up over it. If I'd checked the police reports and his story more carefully, I would have realised he couldn't have got from his flat to Love Lane four minutes after being called, not unless he'd smashed the world record for two-thousand metres. He was there watching from the start.'

'I should be more careful who I go to bed with,' she said.

'Speak of the devil…' said Tom, pointing towards the mine. A figure had come down off the moor and was walking along the track towards the entrance.

'I'm going in for him,' said Tom.

'No – the police told you to stay here. Leave it to them.'

'Sorry, I can't do that. I want to give him the bad news *personally*,' said Tom, opening the door of the car and quickly getting out. Amelie tried to pull him back but it was too late, he was gone.

The inside of the mine was pitch-black but at the far end of the tunnel, Tom could see a man with a flashlight crouching over a large package.

'It's a concrete gnome from a garden centre and it cost twenty-quid,' said Tom as he walked up towards the shadowy figure. 'Nice to see you again Detective Tallis.'

Rob Tallis stood slowly up and turned around.

'Well if it isn't Sherlock fucking Holmes,' said the policeman. 'I should have finished you when I had the chance.' Tallis nodded to himself as if realising, too late, how he'd been lured into the trap. He turned to look down at the package and shook his head, 'I don't have a garden to put this in so I may as well be heading off.'

Tallis moved towards Tom who stood barring the way.

'I swear I'll do you this time if you don't step aside,' the detective said.

'But we have to wait for your fellow police officers to arrive. You won't know them - they're from outside the county and they don't like bent coppers. I think I can hear them coming now.'

Tallis lunged forward and grabbed Tom, throwing him down to the ground. The two men rolled across the floor and into the wire fence around the old shaft, pushing it over as they fell back on to the timber boards which covered the top of the mine. Tallis caught Tom with a heavy blow to the side of the face then reached across and lifted up the grinning gnome before bringing it down towards Tom's head. A second before the lethal load connected, Tom rolled away, sending the statue and Tallis splintering through the rotten timber and into the shaft below.

For a few seconds, Tom lay in the semi-darkness, breathing heavily, before crawling away from the edge of the black hole. He could see flashlights at the tunnel entrance and called out.
'I'm here – I'm alright...'
A group of policemen filled the tunnel as Amelie rushed forwards and knelt down beside him.
'He was right about one thing, being roughed-up is getting to be a habit,' he said, looking up at her and smiling.
'Where's Detective Tallis?' said a police sergeant, walking up to Tom.
'Shafted,' said Tom, pointing to the open mine.
'I thought we told you to stay in your car,' said the policeman, unamused.
Tom looked up at them both, shrugged, and then painfully tried to sit up. 'I think I've *really* buggered-up my back this time,' he said.

Chapter Twenty-One

Never to be Sold

It was early October when Tom found himself once again driving across the West Penwith peninsular with the roof down. Although the sun was still bright, the air was fresh and autumnal as he came in through the outskirts of Polporth but this time, instead of turning down the hill towards the harbour, he took the high back-road which ran above the town and would bring him to the art gallery. Although small, the Polporth Collection included works by many great artists – all of whom had been inspired by the coastline and the special quality of the Cornish light.

Tom left the *Thetis* in the gallery car park then walked down the steps which led to the tall, white, entrance rotunda. He went in through the set of thick glass doors, up to the desk and then, with a small paper sticker for his lapel and armed with a floor plan and a catalogue, walked along a stone-flagged corridor, past a double-height stained-glass window and up to the galleries.

As well as the permanent collection, a new exhibition was staged here every three months. The current show was called

'*Silver Light - Photographs of the coasts and rivers of Cornwall*' and as
he walked up the stairs, he made a mental note to return to
see it before he left. But it was the *Recent Acquisitions* display
that he was seeking, in particular, the space which, just a
month ago, had been added for one new, special arrival.
He followed the signs up to the top floor, walked through
the gallery and then slowly, respectfully, into the small dark
side-room like a pilgrim entering a holy place.

Desire was not in a case as he had expected but was set on a
thin oak plinth mounted on a waist-high pedestal and lit by a
single white beam of light from above. The pale marble
figure was just two-feet high but the detailed working of the
material and the fineness of girl's features made her look
alive. Four other people stood quietly in the room with him
and after a minute or two in one place, each would walk
slowly to a new position as if they were all part of a subtly
choreographed ballet.
Here was Tessa as she had been. A young woman in love –
her body and face full of yearning as she reached out to
embrace her invisible Anton. Only once before had Tom
been moved in this way by a work of art. It was the first time
he had seen the Da Vinci *Virgin and Child* 'cartoon' in
London and it too had its own room, the lighting dimmed to
preserve the delicate charcoal and chalk medium. But that
had been a Great Work - he had expected to be changed by
it. *Desire* was surely too modest a piece to have such an effect
and yet here, in this provincial gallery by the sea and in front
of a simple portrayal of longing and tenderness, he felt the
same sense of wonder.

He walked around her twice then went across to look at the
small card on the wall. It read:
'*Desire*', *Carrera Marble, Anthony Maier.*

On permanent loan to the gallery through the generosity of Ms Tessa Varle.'

He was happy. In the end, they had all found their way home. Then, as he turned to leave, a hand touched him on the shoulder. It was Tessa.

'You're beautiful,' he said, gesturing towards the statue then looking at Tessa's lovely and now somehow less troubled face. 'It's wonderful to see you.'

'Thank you for bringing her back to me,' she said.

'She's been an important part of both our lives.'

'And now she's free, out in the world. I come to see her every day,' said Tessa as she looked lovingly at the sculpture. 'Come back to see *me* one day Tom.'

'I'd like to.'

'One day soon then,' she said.

Back in his car, Tom put the catalogue on the front seat beside him and thought again about the sculpture and the woman whose love had helped make it.

He picked up the book and turned to the page about *Desire*. There were images of the maquette, a short section on its history and a photograph of Anthony Maier as he had been in life – handsome and strong and so sure of who he was. Tom began to read the text, part of which had been taken from the dead artist's last interview:

'Is it a lonely life? Yes it can be…like sailing alone to an uncharted island at the edge of the world to look for buried treasure. It's a hard journey, but worth it if you bring something back which makes us better than we were before.'

Tom started-up the *Thetis* and pulled away. He was going back to a demanding case load but there was a holiday with his children to look forward to and there were things he wanted to say to Amelie. It would be an interesting time.

As he drove out of Polporth, he stole a farewell glance back across the bay. The sun was going down now, its last rays catching the tops of the breaking waves and lighting-up the fronts of the houses along the quayside. He imagined Tessa leaving the gallery to climb the green hill and sit alone by the chapel overlooking the sea. Then he hid his sadness with a smile and thought of the road ahead.